MENTAL HOARDING

Copyright © 2017 by Steve Bonham

Printed in the USA.

Cover Design and Interior Format

© THE KILLION GROUP INC.

MENTAL HOARDING

A
FIFTY YEAR
COLLECTION OF
NON-DISPOSABLE
THOUGHTS

STEVE BONHAM

DEDICATION

There are 7,500,000,000 people in the world. Of those 7.5 billion, only 2 call me "Dad". They've been the best I could have hoped for. Sending my love to:

My son Caleb and his wife Crystal
My daughter Aly and her husband Isaac

TABLE OF CONTENTS

INTRODUCTION

Those poor hoarders. No matter how big their house is, crap litters the floor. Literally. Crap.

Junk is stacked to the ceiling, their yard is overgrown, the toilet hasn't been flushed since Madonna was popular and the five-month old cheese sitting on the counter is next in line for a haircut.

It's a tough thing for those in normal society to understand. For the hoarder, however, any and every possession on the property is valuable. That chair in the corner with only two legs left? Well, it's a "must keep" of course. After all, the hoarder has plans to someday whittle a couple of legs out of the dead tree which graces the front yard. So why throw away a perfectly good chair?

As for that stack of newspapers ten feet high in the master bedroom? The hoarder can't toss those either because there's some information on the Watergate break-in they might need to bone up on. You never know when additional information on the role of G. Gordon Liddy in the crime might come in handy.

Once you see past the piles of cat feces and the skeletal remains of a few mice underneath the couch, you can get into the mind of a hoarder. Simply put, they like their **crap** and are attached to their **crap**. For the non-hoarder though, we like our **stuff** and are attached to our **stuff**.

Stuff. Crap. Not much of a difference. Unless it's mixed in with seven year old cat poop. Then it's definitely crap.

In truth, we are all hoarders of something. The rich hoard money, politicians hoard favors, inmates hoard cigarette butts and, like a squirrel hoarding nuts for the winter, Bill Clinton hoards condoms.

As for me? I hoard my thoughts. I keep them at the ready, always prepared to dispense them to anyone who gives the impression they want to hear what might be going through my brain.

Like what kind of thoughts? If you ask about on-line dating, I have a thought. Or a thousand. How about Russian women, the 80's, World Cup soccer, Easter, minimum wage? Have a seat and let me tell you what's come to my mind regarding those subjects.

Thoughts all over the board and I can't dispense with any of them. Lessons learned from athletics, the role of prayer in life, how to raise a child and the problem with today's colleges. Was Jesus a nerd? Sit down and discuss. Does the government do anything right? No need for discussion, we all know the answer to that one.

Just as the Elvis decanter on the desk is valuable to the hoarder, so my thoughts on "givers-takers" are valuable to me. After all, it's difficult for me to throw them away. I worked hard to become a thinker. Why would I want anyone to drop a dumpster off in my life and discard my thoughts?

It isn't going to happen. Just ask my children, Caleb and Aly. They've been treated to my thoughts their entire life and, knowingly or not, they've helped form a lot of them. Bless their souls as they are probably a bigger part of this book than I ever planned. But they've been with me through it all.

This book is a decent reflection of life. With one set of glasses on, my life has been a letdown. Full of hardship and a ton of undeserved grief. Yet peering through a second set of peepers, I'm one of the most blessed men I've ever known. Great kids who never caused me an ounce of trouble, damn near perfect health my entire life, a sense of humor which kept me laughing since my earliest memory and a rational outlook on life which kept me centered.

While this book isn't my life, it is a brief overview of things I encounter and the thinks I thunk and thinked in a normal day.

"I'm Steve. And I'm a hoarder."
"Hi Steve…"

A mental hoarder anyway. And if you don't like it, please don't plan an intervention for me.
Because I'm keeping all of my stuff.

Well, with the exception of the Elvis decanter. Oh, and the dead cat underneath the futon.

CHAPTER 1

STORING UP FOR WINTER

"Go to the ant thou sluggard; consider her ways and be wise" (Proverbs 6:6)

The 700 square foot apartment wasn't all I could afford. It was just all I wanted. I was deflated. After thirty years and a paid off house, the idea of living in a shared complex bothered me. Surrounded by college kids more interested in beer pong and body shots than creating a future, at fifty-four, the days of apartment living had long passed and I wasn't happy to be a member of the Apartment Community.

Regardless, Apartment 5403 was going to be my home. A moving truck might have transported my stuff to this location, but it isn't what brought me here. An unfaithful spouse did that. For the previous ten years, while I was taking the kids to Little League, she was "working late." As I was diligently preparing our financial future, she was squandering away the trust and love of the family. Year after year.

So, there I was. Like an unaware driver starting a chain reaction of accidents on the freeway, once the dominos of adultery started to drop, they fell fast. My family quickly fragmented, the job I knew for nearly thirty years was lost, insurance policies were cancelled and lifelong friends and acquaintances faded into the sunset. Adding the ultimate insult to the diligence and loyalty I had provided my family, the paid off house was acquired by the one who cheated.

Enter Apartment 5403.

The life I knew for thirty years quickly bore no resemblance to the life I now called my own. Like a man violently hit in the head with a foreign projectile, I was dazed and stunned. I could not understand how my life, which had been committed to making the right choices, had gone south in such short order. The wheels of devastation set in motion by the actions of someone else.

A loser I was not. In fact, my resume and accomplishments would be quickly accepted by most people in America. How did things go so bad? Aren't loyalty, hard work, responsibility and good decision making supposed to save you from troubled times? Truth be told, I had done little, or nothing, to create this lot in life.

Then I realized. Maybe I was just a victim of time and chance.

The good book tells us that "time and chance happen to us all." Innocent fish get trapped in nets, guiltless birds are caught in windmills and decent men and women end up in 700 square foot human kennels through no fault of their own.

Looking at my situation, you'd assume I was the spouse who had wrecked the family. In this story, however, I was the one who had kept it together. "What did I do to deserve this Lord?" I would cry out. Yet I knew that if God didn't care while the ruin of the family was happening, He wasn't likely to care much now.

While in Apartment 5403, I could never escape a troubling thought. "I'm serving the prison sentence for a crime I didn't commit." No matter what encouragement I received from friends, I knew the truth.

The truth and unwavering knowledge is that good things in life aren't always handed out accordingly. Decent people are robbed, loyal spouses are betrayed and healthy eaters are killed in accidents. The occurrence of bad things doesn't mean you're the cause. It just means you might someday be a victim of time and chance and for some unlucky people your next stop in life is Apartment 5403. As for the lucky people, those who stored up for tough times, they too can end up in Apartment 5403 and they'll never be happier.

Also found in the apartment, were my two grown children. They visited me frequently. After the divorce, their love for me grew and the relationship we shared was solidified. Watching me persevere as I worked through my challenges has taught them life lessons they would have never learned otherwise. Inside the apartment also dwelt peace. I finally lived in a non-abusive dwelling and wouldn't have traded in the 700 square feet for the 3000 square feet I lost in the divorce.

"Better a dry crust with peace and quiet than a house full of feasting with strife," I remember being taught in Sunday school. The verse is now written prominently on my whiteboard. The feast of material blessings has not fully returned to my life, but the signs of spring are evident. I know, soon, the summer of my rebuilding is coming.

Winners will continue to be winners. In life's game, they don't win every quarter. Might not even win every half or game. By the end of the season though, they are always in the chase for the championship. Always in the chase that is, because of earlier preparation.

Proverbs tells us to consider the ant and be wise. Wisdom is gained through the observation of ants? Admittedly, I've searched a ton of places to gain wisdom. Through the years, I've read too many books on leadership to count. I've listened intently to motivational speakers, worshiped at the feet of championship coaches, picked the brains of self-made millionaires, devoured powerful quotes from history and religiously watched every episode of Shark Tank. Now, at fifty plus years of life, I'm told that wisdom is found in the ant? Pray tell! I'm all ears.

In considering the ant, we need to take note of its behavior before challenging times burst onto his scene. Not waiting for challenging times to come, the ant prepares for the winter by storing up in the summer. Now there's a novel idea. Knowing that tough times will eventually be presented, the ant thinks ahead. Or thinks with his head. Or what-ever. All we know is that the ant is often smarter than we humans are. It actually thinks three or four stages ahead. Always the giver, I'm here to help. We too, can store up for the winter which is bound to come.

When I was fifty, Apartment 5403 was the dream of some California real estate investment company. Four short years later, it became my refuge during a personal winter." Thankfully, I had considered the ant and been somewhat wise. I had mentally hoarded wise thoughts, memorized sound biblical verses and had built a strong foundation gleaned from the teachings and encouragement of those around me. Acquaintances in my life faced similar winters:

"My dad, literally, played Russian roulette in front of us when we were children."

"My mom kicked me out of the house the day after my high school graduation. I packed my car, with all of my possessions, and headed to nowhere."

"My husband left for a trip and never came home. He never even said goodbye."

"My daughter is a meth addict, living on the streets and I don't know where she is."

Some people in life enjoy a San Diego winter. Others are enduring an Antarctic, never-ending, record setting level winter.

By human standards, the ant is behind the times. He wears horrible clothing, rarely takes a bath and never applies deodorant. In other words, most ants would fit in nicely at a Burning Man festival. But we digress.

Yet, despite lagging behind humans in most areas of life, the ant gets it when the conversation turns to facing known and impending challenges. As humans, we too can store up for winter. We can build character. Live with confidence. Use our brains to plan for success and execute that plan.

How are the successful made? How do we live with vision, resolve and play from a position of strength? If you're already living with these traits, then you're storing up for winter. It's surviving, but not limited to surviving. It's surviving well.

I knew him well. He was a really good guy. A great family man, employee and neighbor. He did damn near everything right. His reward was a golden life. He was content and breathed in his good fortune. Yet, for some reason, time and chance had other plans for him. His life soon came crashing down. Through no doing of his own, the strong winds of fate led to a tornado. The tornado became a hurricane and the hurricane led to the tsunami.

"He's strong," they said. "He'll survive." To which I asked them, "He may survive. But will he survive well?"

Surviving well. That's the key. People survive auto accidents. They survive heart attacks and they survive the death of loved ones. But they don't always survive well. They are simply the non-fatal statistics, living emotionally paralyzed until eternity.

Just because someone survives, it doesn't mean they survived well. It just means the test didn't kill them. Check their pulse often.

You may be the difference between them surviving well or succumbing to the tsunami.

CHAPTER 2

THE MISSING MANUAL
POINTERS FOR PARENTS

~~~~~~~~~~~~~~~~~~~~~~~~~~~~~~~~~~

If the old proverb, "It takes a village to raise a child," is true, carefully examine what the village is teaching. Then pay close attention to how much of it they're teaching. After all, no matter how hard they try, it's not the job of the village to raise your child.

Take the productive lessons from the village and discard the rest. You'll do well if you align the fruits of your loins with a great teacher, a wise coach, a loving family and you buy a house in a superb neighborhood. Surround your child with excellence and morality and good things are bound to happen. That's the part of the village you keep.

Sadly, however, the village, too often, offers a lot of smelly manure. Okay, the stench lives in D.C. and we vote them into office every four years, but I'm getting off point. If I would have given the village free reign in raising my children, my daughter would have been wearing a thong at three, shaking her booty at six, rolling her own at ten and becoming the victim of something by fourteen.

Do yourself a favor and make child-rearing easier. Throw away most of the music produced by the village and don't watch their trashy movies. None of it will help your child find greatness. They will learn, however, every slang term for penis known to man and where to score a dime bag within minutes. Avoid cowardly political correctness if you value strength and courage. The village is pathetically weak and lacks common sense. Thus the need for college courses in human sexuality. The village needs to be taught what comes natural to every farm animal on Earth. And, for crying out loud, steer clear of the colon cleansing members of the village. They'll just give you diarrhea and blame it on capitalist greed.

I'm thankful I didn't let the village raise my children because it doesn't replace parenting. Nor should it. While it takes a lot of good people to get the job done, the appropriate and positive direction which should be provided to our young people must be offered by loving and competent role models.

It's long been a trite and overused line from parents. "When I had my children, they didn't come with an instruction manual."

Of course not. Of the many things flying out of Mom's body during childbirth, a soft cover how-to-book is not one of them. Good thing too. If a manual were to come shooting out of Mom's nether regions, it would probably be pretty slimy and unreadable. Similar to anything Larry Flynt ever published.

Yet parents continue to use the excuse to their unrealized detriment because when they bemoan that a manual is required for proper child rearing, they're silently admitting they're clueless and unable to lead their little nose miners toward good behavior.

Thank goodness a manual does exist in the form of wisdom from those who have raised children. Wisdom gained over centuries and still relevant today. Who needs a library on raising children when a potpourri of parenting pearls are porously presented persistently?

So to the parents of young toddlers, here's a sampling of the pearls you'll receive in this chapter: Let your babies cry a little at night. They'll be fine. In twenty years, no one on the globe will come running to their rescue when they feel insecure.

Keep them out of the adult bed. If your goal is to prepare them for the real world, slobbering on Mom's boob all night for the first seven years of their life isn't going to get the job done. If you want them to be close to boobs their entire life, just teach them to align themselves with politicians. Otherwise, the adult bed is for things adult. Let the rug rats develop some toughness and independence in the comfort of their own bed.

To the parents of pre-teens and teens. You ask, "How will my youngsters behave during their high school years?" Here is my most educated answer: On balance. If you want a window into how your child will act as a teenager, look no further than how you acted at that age. If you drank young, expect booze to be in their canteen by the time they take general math. Did you experiment with sex long before you experimented with petri dishes in science? Start clipping coupons for diapers now. That's where they're likely headed. Unless, of course, you follow the tips outlined in this book. In that case, you'll go a long way in setting your youngsters on the right path!

No official manual is needed. That's an old cop out. Following the insight discussed below will help you avoid disaster and you'll be able to have sex in your own bed without having to share the boobs in the room.

This chapter also isn't limited in "How To" advice aimed at raising the youngster. It also contains helpful hints on how the parent can sharpen themselves in the pursuit of becoming the best they can be as well.

For example, a few years ago, I created an exercise that has become a hit with people who seek my opinion and guidance on parenting. Here is what I challenge them to do. Write down the top five things missing in your life and which you want to acquire. Material wishes (i.e. cars, vacation homes, and trophy wives) are not appropriate, only things with lasting value (i.e. close bond with siblings, religious faith and….wait for it…trophy wives).

Invariably, after they prioritize their top five wishes, people notice the list consists of items they once had but voluntarily gave up. They remember resigning from that job they now regret leaving. They recall booting a date to the curb and now realize their mistake. Married people cheat and then lose the very person they once knew was a gift from God. They also overspend, losing the money they now wish they had.

We voluntarily give up time with our children, lose our physical fitness and forfeit our valued and hard earned reputations. Many people lose (what they now value) through a conscious choice, personal neglect or a simple greed for more. What was once theirs is now gone. Why do we willingly give up people, blessings and things, only later to realize their value and then wish for their return?

What's on your list right now? How many things do you now seek which were once a part of your normal life and you voluntarily gave them up?

The moral of the story? If you value what you have, be content. You may regret losing it if you don't safe guard it. As someone once said, "Don't risk what you can't afford to lose."

PREPARING FOR CHILDREN

The best time to prepare for raising your children is years before you have them. In short, prepare yourself. It's going to be tough to give your kids something you don't possess so mold yourself with the character and moral traits needed for success.

Gentlemen. It's not a hard concept to understand. Your children will watch your every move and hear your every word. They will see how you treat their mother, how you interact with your neighbor and will absorb your every vibe. Whether you like it or not, they will get you. Similar to blaming your flatulence on the dog. You won't have them fooled. Therefore, get yourself together in advance.

After eighteen years of immersion into what is called "Dad," your little girl will have learned from you what to seek in a man. Here's the formula you should expect:

What you are *as* a man = What she'll expect *in* a man

And your little guy will have formed his style after what you taught him.   Here's the formula you should expect:

What you *are* as a man = What he'll *be* as a man

Measure precisely and aim high. You only get one shot at it.

And don't blame your gas on Rover. Your sleight of hand doesn't work when the dog died eight years ago.

Here's another <u>Tip of the Day</u>: Whatever you do, don't make your kid a survivor!

Too many people survived their childhood. They didn't enjoy it. They survived it and became great people despite their lackluster upbringing. Surviving rotary dial telephones, the Osmond's and polyester slacks is one thing. Surviving child abuse in a praise-less and critical home is quite another. They became great anyway. They survived well.

They aren't great because they were loved. They are great because they survived well after being unloved. They aren't great because they were born with a silver spoon. They are great because they survived well being totally neglected. Thankfully, they never bought into the idea that childhood is something to be survived and they'll pass that knowledge onto future generations. Their kids won't be survivors because they won't need to be.

There's nothing more inspirational in life, than to hear the victorious story of the survivor. Unless it's the beautiful story of a person who never needed to become one in the first place.

Before you have children, be sure you're an encourager, always building up and taking advantage of opportunities to inspire. It's often so simple as to be absurd. Do you have three seconds in your day?

Then you can be an encourager.

We approached each other in the hall. I'd never seen her before and said, "Good morning." She responded in kind and within three seconds, she complimented me. What kind of person had I encountered? Was she wanting a part of the big guy? But if she wasn't hitting on me, why else would she offer up a compliment for no reason?

Actually, it was none of the above and all about who she was and what I had been conditioned to expect. You see, in the eighteen years I had lived at home growing up, I don't remember a compliment from my father. Maybe one slipped past every five years or so. Maybe even every leap year or at the sighting of Halley's Comet. I simply don't remember one. Suffice it to say, I was never in danger of drowning in a sea of praise while at home.

Truth be told, I finally arrived at the point of not caring either. I always knew good people existed. People who genuinely possess love and kindness. I realized I wanted to be different from my father. So I formed the Three Second Club. No, it's not a club made up of men who have no staying power in bed. That's the Three Minute Club. It's an attitude of showing the power of what can be accomplished in three seconds.

Do in seconds what others couldn't achieve in decades. Compliment someone. Build them up. It's what leaders do, what givers exude and the moment parts of your character spills forth.

The Three Second Club has unlimited member-
ship. Consider joining today! And for you fellas
in the Three Minute Club, just pray you have an
understanding partner.

Children long for your approval and that craving
will, in all likelihood, last a lifetime. No matter how
old or accomplished they become.

A tearful and aged football player couldn't have
been any clearer. He had reached the pinnacle of
football achievement with his induction into the
Pro Football Hall-of-Fame. Humbly and quietly speaking of the honor years later, he revealed
what it meant to him. All of his accomplishments
in college and professional football were proof to
his father of how good he had become. Becoming
"the man" in college was great, but it didn't appear
to quench the thirst of pleasing his dad. Years in
pro football of being one of the best at his position didn't seem to do it either. The proof to his
father of his prominence in athletics came when
he scaled the highest peak the sport has to offer.

Children need the approval of their parents and
the lengths they'll go to in their pursuit of it will
astonish you.

You'll do well to lift up your children and you'll do
ever better when you display composure and grace
under fire. Do this also before you have children.
Learn to calm the heck down.

Someone once said, "When things start to unravel, don't unravel with them."

Leaders make a decision to be calm under pressure. Always striving to keep their head about them and maintain their wits as their world seemingly crumbled. When things get challenging, leaders make the choice to steam forward through setbacks, trials, pain and rejection.

It's amazing how quickly people give in. They howl, "I quit!" at the slightest bump in the road. Skin so thin you can see bone. They are easily hurt and offended, play the victim card swiftly, surrender when even a marginal effort is required and run if the smallest amount of courage is necessary.

But that's where they are in life. It's not how leaders choose to survive, but the decision belongs to each individual. Somewhere along this path called life, things will unravel. Count on it. It's your decision, however, whether or not you succumb to the challenges presented.

PARENTING DURING THE SCHOOL YEARS

Once your children enter school, you are embarking on some of the most enjoyable and entertaining days you'll ever have. To get through it all, maintain your sense of humor.

Where has the humor gone in our society? I'm constantly offending people with even the slightest display of humor and when I do, I can bet the offended fall into one of three categories: 1) They are passionate about politics, 2) They are uncommonly vocal in stating their opinions or, 3) They missed the prom in high school to study for their college entrance exams.

In the home, have fun! It starts with joking. Playful joking. Like this:

Any true leader knows that playfully ribbing another individual is key to the much needed tearing down of someone's self-esteem. It's also a wonderful tool when trying to manipulate another person, silencing them and forcing them to agree with you.

In a photo gracing my office bookshelf, Aly and I mock our way out of an argument we lost with Caleb, attempting to make him doubt whether or not he's right.

Mocking...55% of leadership coaches recommend it, 35% are opposed and the other 30% don't care. Try it today! One thing to remember though: what you sow is what you'll reap.

Just testing your humor level there. Of course mocking your loved ones doesn't promote tight and loving families. It was a humor check. Real humor, on the other hand, is of extreme value.

While golfing, I tee off. The ball travels, uh, shall we say....inches. Much to Caleb's amusement.

"Did that go backwards, Dad! Haha. How can you swing so hard, hit the ball, and have the ball land behind you?!?!"

The apple doesn't fall far from the tree I guess. In my thirty years of being a parent, I've shared tens of thousands of laughs with my children. They kept me young, healthy in mind, energetic and ever looking forward.

Humor aside, not everything which happens will be knee-slapping comedy. Never lose sight of the fact that your kids are kids. They'll screw up and you'll need to keep an open mind about that. Listen to those who see your children as they are: fallible and full of mistakes.

While coaching, I learned an important lesson early. You can give a parent even the mildest of criticism of their child and they'll never agree with you. Keep in mind, they know you're right. They simply will never acknowledge it. Why not? Because their kids are a reflection of them. Noticing a weakness in the child is pronouncing on the mountaintops the failures of the parent.

Your children are not perfect so never expect people to only see faultlessness in them. Remember all the nefarious stuff you did growing up? That's your kid right there! Maybe you've forgotten what screw-around, brainless youths we all were a few decades ago.

It's 2004 and I'm standing in the receiving line at my mother's funeral. As I greet the visitors, an old lady approaches me. Not a day younger than eighty, she politely says to me, "Little Stevie. I used to babysit you when you were in Kindergarten and I must say...you were quite a little troublemaker!"

I say nothing but am thinking, "Yeah right, you old fart. You don't even know that ruby red lipstick doesn't go with that neon purple hat you're wearing"

Right after I finish my defensive and juvenile thoughts, a second old woman approaches and says, "You must be Steve. I was your Sunday school teacher when you were five, and I'll never forget how ornery you were."

I thought, "She's 90 years old. What does she know!" I moved on, not letting my fragile self-esteem be affected by an old lady's memories of decades past. I didn't need to impress her anyway. After all, I had a date that week and her hair wasn't the color of a broken crayon.

I said nothing but was thinking, "I'm beginning to see a pattern here." Forty years later and they remembered clearly some details of when I was young.

Parents, people see your kids and know them better than you think. Listen to them but not too much, after all, you don't want to know everything you kids are doing behind your back! Especially during their teenage years. That can get ugly and embarrassing. We all have stories.

One Friday night my junior year in high school, my brother and I, along with two other unidentified friends, decided on an evening of fun-fun meaning doing many things that JWND. Jesus Would Not Do.

We did things. And more things. Most of which are now exempt from prosecution because of Statute of Limitation laws. We did things until it was early Saturday morning stuff. And we're not talking 1:00 a.m. Saturday morning stuff. We're talking, "Oh crap!!! We got to get home!!!" Saturday morning stuff.

When my brother and I finally arrived home that morning, we straggled into the house and immediately saw our Dad sitting at the table, reading the paper. "Oh Lord!" we thought. "How are we going to explain being gone all night? We've hacked off the old guy so may as well let the punishment commence. We are so busted!"

Thankfully, Dad was both trusting and naïve on this occasion, briefly setting aside his customary critical nature. He glanced up from reading the paper, looked at us with his patented scowl and said, "Wow. You boys got out of bed early this morning."

"Yes, we did, Dad" was my brother's reply, as he looked at me and grinned. Knowing we had just pulled one off on the college professor.

It's a struggle growing up. We all remember the challenges. Acne, voice changing, body changing, high school cliques, college choices. Hearing "YMCA" on the radio every hour, on the hour. That alone was enough to ruin a kid's childhood.

There's nothing easy about it. At no time in your life do you change more than the years you spend in school. Parents, knowing your child is facing a different challenge on a daily basis, see what you can do to ease some of the pain. Support them.

The rigors of college basketball were testing Aly. It was a daily drain on her. I heard it in her voice, saw it in her face and was concerned.

Since I was a thousand miles away, my options were limited in what I could offer. So I decided I had one card to play. I could be a gift of encouragement. I could help her "walk on the sunny side of the street." So *every* morning, I made sure Aly had an uplifting text from me when she woke up. I'd write it the night before and send it deep into the night. The first thing she saw every morning was a loving, encouraging note from someone who was thinking of her.

Daily practice was a beat down for the players, physically and emotionally. Coaches at the collegiate level are there to win, not foster a positive environment. So your having-fun level is not high on their list of priorities. If a player wants encouragement, it'll need to come from an outside source. Much like life in general.

I still make sure those close to me get reinforcement from me. Just a brief note or quick call to let them know I believe in them. Or simply encouraging them to reach their potential. Nothing fends off discouragement faster than a daily dose of support. Like this:

Back when the kids were in school, I'd type out a note, stick it in an envelope and put it in their lunch. At first, I wasn't sure how they would receive it. Would they be embarrassed and secretly read the note when hiding under the table? Would the other kids find out about the 'secret missives' and bully my kids causing them a lifetime of therapy and the right to claim victim status? Would they then be courted by Jerry Springer for an appearance during "Bullied Kids: They're Doomed Forever" Week?

Thankfully, reasoned heads prevailed and I kept with the plan. Try it. Write a note, pack it in their lunch and trust it was the right thing to do. I'd write something funny, encouraging, thought provoking or simply extend an invite to do something fun together.

Years later, the children still remember the notes. I even ran across some of them a few days ago. One had even acquired some coffee stains along its journey, a journey whose days belong to the ages. But the notes to a couple of young children remain. They served their purpose.

The purpose of helping two young people in little Fort Collins, Colorado know someone was thinking about them that day. Thinking and doing. I've never believed in quality time over quantity time. Too often, the following sounded like an excuse:

"Yeah. Sadly, because of my eighty hour work weeks pursuing my passion, I don't see little Johnny very much. Maybe a couple of times a month. But when we do spend time together, it's quality time!"

Color me skeptical that the absence of quantity equates to quality. Here's a case for quantity time:

Worn tires build healthy bonds. Maybe I can coin that, even though no one knows what it means. Worn tires don't happen when you're lying on the couch. It only happens with effort and intent.

I've been a runner for three decades. In that time, I've run with elite runners from all over the country. From Olympic gold medalists to college All-Americans. But none of them rate with my little running buddy. Well, she didn't start as a running partner. She started on wheels.

When she was really young, Aly would get on her little bike and peddle next to me on my runs, her tiny legs laboring to finish three or four miles. Our conversation was basic, never really getting too much depth. The runs/rides weren't about depth. They were about bonding.

As noted, I've never subscribed to the quality time argument. Quantity is equally important. In this case, massive amounts of time together between a runner and a little girl peddling as long as she could. Just to be with her father. As I write this morning, she is now in her late 20's and the bonding worked. Our relationship is the best it's ever been.

The bike now hangs in the garage. The tires worn and without tread. It's one of the most valuable bikes in Colorado. For it was worn out through miles and miles of relationship building.

Raise your children with no regret because, like the changing of the seasons, your time with them will end before you fully realize it.

IT'S OVER:
THE EMPTY NEST AND MEMORIES

This night, the reflection of the Jefferson Memorial shines brightly on the lake. You can see its lights on the water, mixed in with the reflection of the moon. It's a pleasant December evening in 2014 and Caleb and I sit on a park bench. It hasn't been a particularly great year for either of us. On this night, Caleb needs to work through a few issues. I'm grateful to be with him during the holiday season and able to lend an ear.

Just a few short years ago, the questions used to be, "Daddy, when man landed on the moon, could you see him up there?" Or, "Daddy, are the boobs on girls for the baby or for the husband?"

But the hands of time moved at propeller speed and the little boy grew into a man. Since then, the conversations have become quite different. Complete with questions at an advanced stage. We now discuss the possibility of high finance and try to make sense out of life's challenges. We make each other laugh. After all, as we sit on the park bench tonight, we're just trying to make it in this world gone crazy and attempt to create a path for success in the upcoming year.

We take a few seconds and look at the moon in hopes of spotting a man up there. He's not to be found and we admit that the boobs on a girl serve many purposes but the boobs in Washington D.C.

have little value.

At the end of the evening, Caleb walks way a richer man for having spent another hour of his life with his father under the manless moon. His father walks away realizing, yet again, the never ending worth of the willingness of a park bench to seat two grown men still running life's race.

Parenting is forever. As quickly as raising your children begins, it is over. Today's sounds become tomorrow's echoes.

The hoop sits idle in my backyard. Its purpose has been fulfilled. When I bought it years ago, my children eagerly awaited its appearance on our backyard court. Once installed, hardly a day went by in which it wasn't used. Much to the chagrin of our unathletic and non-supportive neighbors, the sound of a bouncing basketball became a common occurrence.

Now, the children who once played on this court have graduated from college and are living on their own. They have moved on to new and more adult interests. The hoop now goes months without being used and, although the children are now grown and gone, if you listen hard enough, it's easy to hear the dribbling of the ball and the excited laughter of children's competition. Noises of times past.

As for the hoop I purchased years ago? Realization of times present. The photos I took of the kids years ago are similar to the shots young families are taking today. I'm on the other side of that mountain and will never regret I chose quantity.

Quantity also builds traditions. You know, traditions are the things we do, decide we like, do it more, then decide we're going to keep doing them. They are the things that span generations.

"Daddy, after dinner, let's play a game," she said. Visions of years gone by exploded into my memory. Except tonight, she's my 27 year old daughter and requesting that we turn back the clock a bit and simply play. Play a game.

We started playing games only a small child could understand. It involved counting and she always tried to cheat. I was so proud. "If you aren't cheating, you aren't trying," I dutifully coached her.

Now, our card games include adult themes and intermittent coarse language. It never grows old. We've done this since she was two and I have no plans to stop anytime soon. So I'll cherish another roll of the dice tonight, knowing that our time together is as sand flowing through the hourglass.

And I'll eagerly await the next announcement from a familiar voice when it says with authority, "Daddy, let's play a game." After all, it's a tradition.

Develop traditions which will be passed down to your children and maybe even inherited by others. After all, isn't that what many holidays are about?

Just think of the traditions passed down through the generations which you obtained from others. On your own, would you have ever dreamed of killing a turkey, filling it's insides with food and insisting you eat it the last Thursday in November while watching football? Ah, the traditions we accept from others!

"Throw me the ball" the little boy said as he ran from his house and into the street where Caleb and I have tossed a football for nearly two decades.

Going outside and throwing the ball. A tradition started when Caleb was young and has extended into his adult years. We talk about everything when we throw the ball. Talks over the years ranging from his childhood friends, teachers he didn't like and if Elway would ever win a Super Bowl.

As he became a man, we still threw the ball. But the in-between-passes discussions grew in importance. We discussed his college major, girls he became interested in, how he could finance a car, why his mother and I needed to get a divorce and whether or not he should take a job in DC.

The world changed over two decades but throwing the ball remained. In the sweltering summer heat, through many rainstorms, fighting the chill of the blowing snow and through the falling of the autumn leaves. Sometimes we'd throw for an hour, other times, for five minutes. We would always find the time to fit in some throwing and some good conversation.

No matter where we were, we threw the ball…and talked…and learned from each other.

I rarely said "not now" whenever Caleb asked, "Dad, want to throw the ball?" because I always knew that throwing the ball was more than an activity. It was father/son bonding. It was an exploration into each other's mindset, opinions and current well-being.

So, a few months ago, when the youngster next door asked us to throw him the ball, I was reminded of the boy who ran pass patterns on the same street in the 1990's and how much value was created by such a simple exercise.

The ball has traveled with us, been left outside and no longer holds air but that hardly means our days of throwing the ball are over. In fact, numerous additional discussions and victories await us in the future because of this one activity.

So here you go little man who lives next door. The torch has been passed and may you get as much out of throwing the ball as Caleb and I have over the years. When you become a Daddy in the year 2029, make sure you make time to throw the ball with your youngsters.

You'll be better for it.

Raising my children was the greatest experience I ever had. The years were full of excitement, laughter and mutual growth. While I never feared them growing older, I did have concern about the empty nest. The empty nest which is now my reality. Nowadays, I look back on the children when they were in my home:

> *They were a joy to raise.*
> *They will never leave me.*
> *They will never betray me.*
> *They will always bring honor to my family.*
> *It has been a rewarding ride to be sure.*

The same can be yours if you cherished every moment you had with them and had no regrets. For most, you've been to heaven together and been sentenced to hell for a time and through it all, you grew closer and proved what family love is about.

MINDLESS MINUTIA:

- Good men of character, honor, integrity and faithfulness make a Father. Lacking these qualities quickly makes a guy little more than someone who simply relieved himself sexually.

- It takes you an hour to invite someone into your life yet it might take months or years to fully remove them if they aren't a good fit with where you want to go. The same applies to your children. Help them choose their friends and monitor closely. You can save them a lot of growing pains if you do.

- I don't know if this is the wisest, saddest or most accurate quote I've heard on the subject of divorce. A highly intuitive female friend summed up her marriage and subsequent divorce: "We spent our entire marriage accumulating the things we would eventually fight for during the divorce."

- Note to self: Never, and I say never, take your millennial aged son to the store with you to pick out and buy a couple of cantaloupes.

- Love the friends of your kids. They bring untold joy. Back when my daughter was in high school, one young man decided to describe me to her. Here's his observation: "Aly, the best way to describe your Dad...he's like a cartoon character."

- I'm guessing he wasn't referring to Superman or Hercules.

- There it is. Right there in Ecclesiastes. "There is a time for everything and a season for every activity under the heavens." It goes on to say, "a time to weep and a time to laugh, a time to love and a time to hate, a time to tear down and a time to build." You get the point.

After raising a girl and a boy, I'm fairly sure those verses should have read:

"A time to hit the toilet and a
time to go all over the floor"

"A time to tell Dad about a new boyfriend
and a time to discuss anything else"

"A time to cry and a time to actually
avoid even trying to manipulate Dad"

"A time to wear sweatpants at home
and a time change into a mini-skirt
after I'm out of Dad's sight"

"A time to ask Dad for money and
a time to ask him for more"

"A time to borrow Dad's car and
never a time to put gas in it"

CHAPTER 3

STEAK EATERS AND BUS RIDERS
THE SUCCESSFUL AND HOW THEY'RE MADE

~~~~~~~~~~~~~~~~~~~~~~~~~~

Leon Fuller had his fill. As the football coach of the Colorado State University Rams in 1984, he had just witnessed his team lose, yet again. On this day, it was a 52-10 defeat at the hands of Air Force.

Fed up with a team who consumed a lot of food before games and rode in fancy buses to the stadium but didn't play hard on Saturdays, Fuller was done and he didn't hold back.

Being interviewed after the game, he told anyone who would listen that too many of his players were merely "steak eaters and bus riders." Coming from your coach, that'll decrease the size of your manhood a bit.

Games aren't won on the college football field with athletes who are more interested in the perks of big time athletics. Pre-game steaks are tasty and the bus rides with your buddies are fun but they don't bring home championships.

You've met those people. Individuals merely along for the ride, attaching themselves to the achievers of the world in hopes of getting a freebie without effort. They are, traditionally, low talent people trying to attach to success. They believe who you know outweighs working to achieve their goals.

They short themselves though, not realizing the taste of victory is sweetest when the taste of the sweat of labor is still present. Championships are never won easily. Nor are victories likely to be won by simply riding a bus or eating a delicious meal provided by someone else.

A lot of work goes into achievement. Just ask those who have achieved.

What you achieve in life is largely up to you. The world isn't fair. Some people are born into rich families and some into poverty. Others are born with exceptional intellectual brilliance and others with a lackluster thinking ability. Some people have nice looks while others are unattractive. It's never going to be fair.

What to do? What to do?

Let's start here. Use the gifts and talents you have. If you're a one-talent person, use it and cultivate it further. If you're a ten-talent person, develop and deliver on all ten. After all, it's impossible for a ten-talent person to use all ten without benefitting someone else.

Maybe you need to find your gift first. With this young man, it started with an early morning phone call in August, 2012.

"Hey, Steve. I want to interview some people at a political rally. I need your opinion on the questions I want to ask." The young man had taken some time off of his low-level and temporary job to pursue his dream. The dream of political journalism. He possessed talent to be sure, but his current position was not satisfying. Nor was it fully utilizing his talents.

So off he went, taking unpaid time-off and trying something he'd never tried before. He filmed, edited the video and posted it to the internet. The subsequent video went viral and was featured on national TV within twenty-four hours and, as they say, the rest is history.

Up to that point, I'd never seen a young kid work so hard to achieve a goal. From driving a government truck in early 2012 to being featured regularly on national television by 2015. Since he was seen as a political pundit, malicious enemies called him every name in the book. They've commented on and wished for his demise. Yet the non-supporters were offset by a large group of inspirational people throughout the country who were with him every step of his journey and offered him their unconditional backing.

Through it all, he kept faith in himself and believed he could fulfill all of his potential. Most importantly, he's never forgotten who he is. A guy unwilling to let his talents wither away and die or settle for being a "steak eater and bus rider."

There's a ton of competition for what you want in life. What does it take to come out on top? Begin by finding your gifts and using them. Here are fifteen ways to take advantage of your every talent:

1. Don't Accept Inevitable Failed Endings

I recently enjoyed drinks with a highly successful business woman. As I picked her brain regarding her wild success with every company she's been with, she mentioned that none of her plans have ever failed. Ever.

"In twenty-five years, not a single plan of yours has ever failed?." I asked. "No," she replied. I inquired as to how that's possible. "Because I don't ride anything out to a failed ending. If it's headed for failure, I make the changes needed to allow success," she said.

That philosophy isn't common in America anymore. We stay in horrible marriages until one of the parties finally dies. We continue to fund the War on Drugs, increase the food stamp rolls, throw more money into welfare and squeeze tightly the same foreign and domestic policies which have yielded the same rotten fruit for fifty years. It doesn't matter that all are headed for failure. Keep on keeping on! There's nothing to see here, nothing to see.

We'll stick with the same dismal education system which is losing ground by the minute to our foreign counterparts. After all, it's the way we do business. Ride it out until it fails and then keep doing it. Hey, it would look bad to make changes now.

My friend doesn't live in a world of riding something out to its failed conclusion and that's why she's winning. All while most Americans run full steam toward the cliff of failure! If you have resolve, success won't be far behind and that confidence will allow you to stay ahead of the game.

2. Play the Game from a Position of Strength

Think about how great we could be if we didn't play from behind. That is, we lose our fitness level and gain weight, forcing us to make drastic changes in our lifestyle just to get even again. We're playing from behind.

We spend more than we earn and live beyond our means. So we either charge our overspending or borrow money from others. We become debtors. We're playing from behind.

We behave poorly and lose our once good reputations, forcing us into damage control and years of rebuilding. We're playing from behind.

We destroy relationships and burn bridges because of our addictions, requiring us to overcome the loss of fine people in our lives who finally give up on us. We're playing from behind.

Don't play from behind. It's demoralizing and a drain on energy. You'll never use your gifts to the fullest from a position of weakness.

Like any good football team, it's better to play with a lead than have to spend half of the game playing catch up. After all, winning is never accomplished by being behind. Eventually, you need to take the lead. So whatever it is that you're behind in, catch up and grab the lead. Once you're in the lead, don't ever forfeit it again.

Quit playing from behind. I know of people who stay in bed, not because they are tired, but because it's too early to get up. That's right and hear it again. They remain in bed because it's too early to get up. In other words, it was way too early to do something productive. So they choose non-productivity. Because it was too early to get up. Playing from behind.

What kind of logic is that? Let's extend the thinking to other areas of life.

"Well doctor, I didn't come see you because the disease wasn't advanced enough."

"Listen, honey, it's too early to see a marriage counselor. Your court case for hiring a hitman to take me out still hasn't gone to trial."

"Naw, it's too early to start looking for a job. I still have $15.31 left in the bank"

If you're not tired, get out of bed. Rejoice you're no longer playing from behind. Take advantage of your talents and gifts.

3. Be a Human Storm Chaser

This discussion, up to this point, has largely been about you. Your gifts, Your talents. Surviving your winter. We all make our choices for our own good and that's important. Yet using our gifts also has an effect on others. Never look past the importance of serving those around us.

It was the hardest rainstorm I'd ever run in. Pouring rain. Every fiber of my clothing was soaked. About a mile from my house, a car pulled over. It's was a friend of mine.

"Can I give you a ride Steve?" she asked. "No thanks," I replied, "I'm happy as a lark running in this stuff."

Seventeen years later, she and I are having coffee together when her phone rings. "Pardon me," she pleasantly says, "But I must get this call. It's someone I help out every week and I've got to hear what he needs."

It then occurs to me. Seeing a need and with the ability and resources to assist, she once rescued runners from rainstorms. Today, she is helping rescue people from life's storms. In seventeen years, she hasn't changed an iota. Forever, she sees the storms and begins thinking of others. It's the DNA that makes up her existence. She's a Human Storm Chaser.

She sees storms brewing in the lives of others and acts accordingly. It's in the core of her being and, after nearly two decades, it's painfully apparent she'll never change. She's simply using the gifts she's been given to their fullest.

4. Understand that Today is the Sum of all of Your Yesterdays

One man sits in his house lonely, broke, dejected, and depressed and lacks the energy to face tomorrow. Why? Because of his previous choices, decisions, attitudes, friend selections, goals and how he tackled the challenges which came his way.

Another man sits in his house with friends and family. He is prosperous, upbeat, and energetic. He eagerly anticipates being productive tomorrow. Why? Because of his previous choices, decisions, attitudes, friend selections, goals and how he tackled the challenges which came his way.

The tale of two men and how they arrived at their current destination. Not in the Twilight Zone. It's in reality.

The life you have today is the sum total of your past choices and decisions. Sprinkle in a rare out-of-your-control event or two and you arrive at today. You drove the car which delivered you to today's destination. Whether good or bad and, while many want to blame someone else for their lot in life, it's most likely something emanating from them.

Ten-talented people know the importance of wise decisions and choices and act accordingly. The man in Apartment 5403 was the recipient of his past choices, even his choice of spouse. Thankfully for him, the sum of those decisions helped him survive life's harsh winter and allowed him to bloom again in life's spring.

5. Have A Vision

Starting today, if you change nothing, where will you be in a year? If you change nothing, where will you be in five years? Here's the deal. If you change nothing, you can reasonably guess your income in five years, who your friend set will be, how healthy you'll likely be and the car you'll probably be driving.

Where's my prize in that box of Cracker Jack? I'm not seeing the beautiful sunset of retirement in that scenario.

As a coach, I've taught my athletes this: You're either getting better or you're getting worse. But you're not staying the same.

Get rid of mediocrity. Envision higher and better. The world doesn't need any more status quo and it sure as hell doesn't need more underachievement. Raising the bar is long overdue. Starting with you.

It's exciting to see the younger generation going "balls to the wall" in their endeavors. I also instructed my players what I had been taught, "Don't settle for second, when first is there for the taking." Stressing the pursuit of first was important because, in my mind, we were always playing for the championship and it was there for the taking.

Never play for a tie. Play to win. The time is now. Don't settle for second. A lack of vision and planning will ensure underachievement. Consider the ant and be wise. Store up the needed tools for success today! It's never too late.

6. Re-write the End of Your Story
There is a youth center in Denver specializing in the treatment of young women needing assistance and direction. If anyone can complain about the hand they were dealt, these young ladies can make a case. Conversely, many of them can testify to throwing away a beautiful hand. Regardless, they reside at the youth center and they're often struggling to re-write the end of their story.

In a world often void of character and lacking a deep foundation of behavioral expectation, the solid leadership involved at the school was obvious. Simply put, they're a rock. Steady and unflappable. The young ladies from the school are a testament to the changed lives being produced daily.

It's "believing in people" at its finest. Trust in someone, sprinkle in some patience, add boundaries and direction and watch young people bloom.

This youth center is a shining example of that. It's like spreading seed and tending to the garden until growth occurs. Few things of value happen overnight. Yet the response of people to positive encouragement will, eventually, yield a bountiful harvest.

Young people will thrive when given the chance, and possibly become ten-talent people. Troubled teens throughout the country are constantly tempted to remain in their previous lifestyles; lives headed for the land of nothing. They can resign themselves to being three-talent kids or a ten-talent kid who tossed aside many blessings and ended up with one-talent instead.

But the young ladies at the school didn't and now, because of their unwillingness to settle for second and a group of talented people lending exceptional leadership, success stories abound.

They made the choice to re-write the end of their stories into a positive one. They did it by the "addition by subtraction."

7. Lose Mediocrity

During the tough economic times this country has been through in recent years, a lot has been written on the survival of private businesses and companies in general. When speaking of business strategy, I've noticed the following:

Those businesses that want to survive cut their budget.

Those businesses that want to succeed cut their mediocre performers.

Cutting your budget **saves** money. Replacing average employees with high achievers **earns** money. The free market will always have room for a quality employee. Unless, of course, you work at a government job. In that case, productivity is replaced by bureaucracy and the mediocre have the ability to rise through the ranks.

"I heard you have a government job, Betsy. It must be nice!"
"It is! I get off at 5:00 and I'm home by 3:30!"

When you quit being mediocre, watch how quickly your paycheck increases. Addition by subtraction in action! Quit overachieving in underachievement!

8. Gain A Right Focus

The locker room at the health club was fairly packed when one of the employees rushed in and began to feverishly mop the floors. Although we all noticed him, only one of us spoke.

Club Member: "You're working like a bat out of hell. What's going on?
Employee: "I gotta get this place clean. Our District Manager is stopping by today"

This time, we all heard it but few of us caught it. Caught what was actually said.

Which is more important? Having clean facilities

for the paying customers or for the District Manager? You see, impressing customers requires a daily and high level intensity for excellence. Impressing the Big Guy requires minimal effort until it's announced he's dropping by.

A ten-talent business wouldn't need to know the head honcho is arriving since their main concern is the customer. Their facilities always look good. Contrast with a lower talent company which values its yearly review with the boss more than the daily review its customers offer.

Maybe that's why they run monthly discounts *every week*.

9. Avoid Narcissism

The mind of a selfish and narcissistic person is an amazing study. They live their life only for them. Their decisions, thoughts and actions are based on their own desires. They betray, lie, cheat, deceive and care not for those they hurt or destroy. Yet here's the irony. After abusing people and burning bridges for decades, the self-centered person finds themselves alone and they don't know why.

Years of "me" and that's all they have left after a few years. "Me."

They don't like being left with only "me." Their friends and family have long bolted, tired of the abuse and neglect. Often, narcissists have numerous quality gifts and talents. Many are ambitious, funny, intelligent and charismatic. Sadly, these gifts play second fiddle to the brutality of narcissism and are ignored as people throw the entire narcissist away. If you've ever been close to a narcissist, you get what I'm throwing down.

So the next time you want the world to revolve around "you," just remember: One day, if you're selfish and have no concern for others, it will!

10. Be Mature in your Thinking

A newly appointed manager of a large organization began his first presentation before his staff. Sadly, in his talk, he fired up the obligatory slide show and for the umpteenth time in their career, the staff was treated to things they learned in pre-school.

Most in the audience were hungry for revenue projections, technology innovation, staff organization and company expansion. Instead, the manager gave cute illustrations about sharing with each other, being kind and not offending others.

Ten-talent people are mature in their thinking and have graduated from building their corporate business models from pre-school illustrations.

This long-time employee, yet fresh at managing a large division had been promoted from the common ranks into an upper level position. In and of itself, that's not unusual. What is alarming is this. Immediately upon his promotion, he enrolled in a class on leadership.

That's a problem. After a long career in the organization and upon receiving a top-level position, his lack of leadership qualities are admitted the day he signs up for training in that area.

Where have the leaders gone? And why are people lacking the skills to lead drawing six-figure salaries to simply manage? When did it become in vogue to hire "yes wo/men" while the true leaders in the organization die on the vine? Better yet, who would you rather work for, a leader or a manager? At the end of the day, which of those two choices are consistently receiving upper level promotions? Be a leader, a person people will want to follow.

And it usually starts by being a mature thinker.

11. Play to Win

The medium size business is directing all of its efforts toward keeping the doors open. Every penny is spent keeping the lights on and the phones active. Long gone are the days they aggressively pursued new heavyweight clients and developed new products.

Simply put, they are playing "not to lose" as opposed to playing "to win." Their days are spent devising ways to hold the creditors at bay and negotiating pay cuts with employees in hopes of securing their labor at a reduced cost. They make no sales calls, develop no new products and do little to pad their corporate resume.

They are trying to avoid a loss, not forcefully pursuing a win. Similar to us:

We stay in the same crappy job we've had for years as opposed to taking a risk and doing what we really enjoy. Security over satisfaction. Playing "not to lose."

We stay in dysfunctional relationships because "it's better than being alone." Playing "not to lose" instead of winning and being confident enough to wait until you find the right person. It's settling over what could have been a life blessing.

We keep the same friend set, even though they no longer challenge us or take us to greater heights. After all, inviting new people into our lives might be uncomfortable and require us to change our attitudes or behaviors. In other words, playing "not to lose." Winners seek a challenge and invite critique. Losers avoid it.

Quit playing "not to lose" and take an aggressive move toward winning. Replace fear with confidence and trade in security for risk. Resign from the losing mindset.

Someone once said, "At every workplace meeting held daily across America, five seats are reserved for cowardice and no seats are reserved for courage." Why? Because people run scared. Scared to talk, to think, to opine. Scared to stand firm to their convictions and that's too often what the boss/organization wants. Weakness from subordinates.

Cowardice is king across our country. Too often

society doesn't appear to encourage strength or boldness. Those who try are often retaliated against. This attitude has given rise to a large collection of cowards. From cheaters, to vandals, sucker punchers, looters, thieves and wife abusers.

Cowardice has become so common in our society. We hardly notice it anymore.

But that doesn't relieve you and I from the responsibility of being strong and courageous. Ten-talent people are tough and shun cowardice. Whether or not it's ever rewarded or honored. They play to win.

12. Breathe in the Good Days
Do you ever look back at times in your life and regret that those days are over? I might be living in those days right now. Not the days of looking back, but the days that are so good that I hope they don't end.

You see, since the first of the year, I have introduced new people into my life. People who get it. I've noticed that people who are comfortable with mediocrity are quickly leaving my field of vision. There are too many Lazy Boy chairs in our homes these days and too few work benches. Too many pairs of flip-flops in our closets and not enough pairs of running shoes. Too much food in our kitchen and not enough will power to push away from the dinner table.

These are great days. If we allow them to be.

Someone once said that if you want to change your life, change the books you read and the people you spend time with. I hope these moments don't end anytime soon. In the meantime, I'm going to savor each day, hoping that the days stretch into years. The Bible says, "As a man thinketh in his heart, so is he." Successful people are positive in their yesterdays, todays and their tomorrows.

13. Listen to What's *Not* Being Said

During your life, you can count on several things. Life won't be fair, good people will be punished while the guilty remain free, boys will stare at girls and gossips will take aim at you. Consistently.

In order to feel better about the gossip and the venom they spew, start listening to what they're not saying about you.

They aren't saying, "He's lazy," "She's a liar, a cheat and a thief," "Chris sleeps around on his wife and is a neglectful father," "Anita beats her children," "Joe has no honor," "Ericka always blames others."

Sometimes, it is encouraging to listen to what people aren't saying about you. Your enemies will pick on things they believe you to be guilty of. They know outlandish gossip and lies will make them look bad. So they avoid it.

Listen to what they aren't saying. It reveals a lot about you! And that's an awesome thing.

14. Embrace Unending Potential

At what age does a person no longer have potential?

Let's face it. You don't see very many motivational speakers brought in by senior living homes to speak to their residents. When's the last time you gave a 90 year old grandparent a motivational speech CD? When you're around people in the twilight of their life, do you ever quote Vince Lombardi and tell them, "Winning isn't everything, but wanting to win is!"?

Say that and the older generation will reply, "Save your speech. We learned fifty years ago that every win in life fades in importance to the point where no one even remembers who won." They're right. Brutal honesty at its finest.

So why do we never speak to an older person about their potential? I'm guessing that society doesn't embrace that they have any. We don't believe they have the prospects of increasing their value any longer.

Sadly, that says more about us as a society than it does the elderly.

15. Raise the Bar

It was a stark realization for me to take on the challenge of pursuing my dreams. The day my 21 year old daughter announced to me, "Dad, I couldn't work where you work for a day."

"Why not?" I asked. She proceeded to list a variety of reasons, including a humorous parallel to a scene in a movie. Sadly, she was dreadfully accurate in her observations. On one hand, I was thrilled she wanted more in a career than what she saw in my possession. On the other hand, I was disappointed in myself that I had not raised the bar. She and I both knew I could do better.

Ten-talent people don't remain stagnant. They may start small, but through drive, vision and unceasing energy, they constantly reach new heights after new heights.

It begins with raising the standard in the small areas of life.

I'm sitting in an elegant restaurant and quickly learning that I need more experience in fine dining. How's that you say? I go to the restroom and, after washing my hands, tell the attendant, "I see that you have no paper towels here to dry my hands."

He looks pretentiously at me and points to a basket. I blush a bit and tell him, "I'm sorry, I thought those were wash cloths."

You don't see this in the fast food arena!

Raise the bar....

MINDLESS MINUTIA:

- If the field you've been planting in hasn't yielded a crop in the last decade, it may be time to try a new field. Or seek more fertile ground. Or purchase better fertilizer. But quit doing the same thing every year and wondering why you have no harvest.

- If people were as hopeful in life as they are when they buy a lottery ticket, they'd see a more fruitful life come their way

- Do more than you dream

- If you're a ten-talent person, each year you won't need to rebuild like in years past. You'll simply need to reload. Your bench will be deep and not deep with average talent. It'll be deep with great talent.

- Is the life of a coward attractive to you? Me neither. Then why do so many choose to live a life of fear? Afraid to speak, afraid to risk, afraid of honesty and afraid to tell the truth. Is the life of a coward one well lived? If not, why do so many embrace it?

- If you want to achieve, it's hard to:
  1. Become intelligent when you never read
  2. Accumulate riches when you overspend
  3. Lead others if you are unwilling to follow

4. Develop a solid reputation when you live recklessly

5. Be at peace when you encourage conflict

6. Have others by your side if you are self-centered

7. Build if you are one who tears down

8. Be grounded when you compromise your values

9. Have strength if you are easily persuaded

10. Achieve if you have no goal

11. Receive a compliment if you have low self-worth

12. Give a compliment if you have low self-worth

13. Build trust when you lie

14. Live a positive life if focusing on the negative

- Never reach your full potential in averageness.

- Never live up to low standards.

- Don't be a high achiev<u>er</u> in low achiev<u>ement</u>.

- Don't excel in incompetence.

- It's okay to get an education in life's struggles, but you don't need to earn a Master's degree in them!

- In the case of government agencies, higher-ups traditionally make decisions based upon their own well-being and the protection of their own self-interest. Risk taking, creativity, innovation and a spirit of self-starter achievement are rarely rewarded in the government atmosphere.

- I just heard a commercial on inventions which carried the disclaimer, "Most inventions are unsuccessful"

- If you want to spark people to greatness and risk taking, that's probably not the ticket. Few viewers are likely to say, "I'll likely be unsuccessful? Sounds great! Where do I send my money?"

- Great people turn significant challenges into ordinary living while small people take ordinary living and turn it into disaster.

- At the end of the day. Take control of your life. Live well. Provide leadership. Avoid the collateral damage of the hurricanes caused by the reckless.

- With each annual graduating class from high school, is the country moving closer to greatness or further away? Are we producing great or average? A lot rides on the answer.

CHAPTER 4

WISDOM FOR YOUR KIDS AND GRANDKIDS (A COLLECTION OF ACHIEVABLE TARGETS)

For twenty-three years, I had children in my house. As is the case with most parents, your life seems to morph into the life of your children. Your daily schedule evolves from being a one-time party animal to watching endless soccer games. Imagine the trade-offs. Exchanging a decadent night of body shots for watching grade school soccer on the local pitch. It's eerily similar to riding in an Indy car one minute and sitting in a horse carriage the next. With the horse making noise and passing gas the entire ride.

Remember parents, life didn't stop. It just changed and it won't ever change back. By the time the kids are raised and you get your life back, the days of beer pong and swinging drunk from the chandeliers are over and there's only one thing left for a wise and learned parent to do.

Pass the torch and impart any knowledge and wisdom you have to the younger generation.

My days of raising children are over. Once I had two, I determined a third wasn't needed and took care of that back in 1989. "First available appointment," I said, trying to be manly in the midst of losing part of my manhood. Snip, snip and we're good. No more kids, only grandkids.

But if I were starting the entire process of childrearing over again, here are twenty-five points of emphasis I'd pass on to my children, with two bonus suggestions thrown in because I'm in a giving mood today!

1. Accomplishment

Shouldn't the praise "Congratulations!" be reserved when respecting the worthy accomplishment of someone else? Shouldn't this word be meaningful and genuine? Why do I ask you ask?

Because I just received a "Congratulations!." What was my significant achievement you wonder? I successfully upgraded a software program from Version 2.1 to Version 3.4. Nothing to be proud of here and certainly nothing worthy of congratulations. Yet the software congratulated me anyway. These people must not be hard to shop for at Christmas.

Thus, the problem. Kids, when you accomplish something, we'll congratulate you. Remember that soccer trophy you were awarded? Every player received one. All of the awards were blue and carried a "1" on them. If it were up to me, you wouldn't have even been awarded a trophy because you weren't very good. Oh quit people! It's called tough love. Or something along those lines but it doesn't matter. Not all of you were 1st nor were you all a Most Valuable Player. You only received those awards to make you feel good about yourself. A feeling, by the way, that is short-term.

Remember your aunt Cathy and the college scholarship she was awarded? She earned that. Very few athletes get that prize. She practiced every day when she was young. Through injury, discouragement, illness, scorn and difficulty. She did what few were willing to do and received her reward. The rule of thumb is this: If it's worthwhile, not everyone will obtain it.

The phony achievements start with empty Kindergarten graduations. Has anyone in history failed to achieve this? If I was chosen to give the commencement at one of these things, it would sound something like this:

"Listen up rug rats. Just because you're wearing a goofy hat and long cape doesn't mean you did anything special. Unless, of course, you think it's special to take tons of naps, read the always difficult Dick & Jane, and avoid soiling yourself several times a day. Truth be told, absolutely everyone graduates from Kindergarten. So let's break this thing up, have a cookie and some lemonade, change your messy Superman underwear and call it a day."

No valuable purpose is served by handing out shallow "Congratulations" or easily earned "Diplomas." Teach your children what real accomplishment is and how to earn heartfelt praise.

2. Adaptability

You've now learned that life is a mix of extremes. If you don't believe what is written above, consider the following. And then ask yourself, "What kind of life would I have if I wasn't adaptable?"

In the last couple of years, I've:

- Run on a trail at 14,000 feet and on Miami Beach, in the same month.

- Worked on a project, sun up to sun down for weeks on end and yet quit on a training run within the first thirty seconds.

- Been told I'm a wonderful parent and been told my children did well in spite of me.

- Been on the doorstep of wealth and on the brink of making nothing.

- Been told I look like Robert Redford and told I look like Lyle Lovett.

- Visited the graveyard of the dead and yet had nary a coffee with my most cherished friends who are alive and well.

- Watched a grown-up throw a childish tantrum

of colossal proportions and also watched a child behave in a grown-up, gracious, courteous and diplomatic fashion.

- Watched moving trucks unloaded as they fill a house after a wedding and watched a different house emptied into moving trucks after a divorce.

- Spent WAY too much time with an arrogant narcissist and spent way too little time with the kindest, most giving and most humble man I've ever met.

- Became connected on social media with former enemies and disconnected on social media with friends.

- Been brushed off by a woman with a felony arrest record and yet welcomed by a woman worth millions.

- Met a capable person who lives well off of money earned by others and met a person working three jobs to ensure she never has to borrow a dime.

As the good book says, 'There is a time for everything under the sun." "Everything" is pretty encompassing. In life, be prepared for many extremes. Because they will surely happen.

3. Aim High
Someone has said, "Those who aim at nothing usually hit the target." and "Those who are going

nowhere usually get there." Aim at something worth hitting. Knowing where you want to go, what it's going to take to get there, and when it is you want to arrive.

Back in the day, when my kids were in grade/middle school, I would have them write down their targets for the upcoming year. I encouraged them to make academic, athletic and personal goals. One year, Caleb gave his usual two minutes of thought and planning, hurriedly scribbled down his goals and handed them to me. Here's what went down:

Caleb wrote..."Be average." I said, "Caleb. I believe your goal in school was to have a 'B' average, not to 'Be average'."

The intention was good. The execution? Not so hot. Clearly defined goals, with deadlines, will do wonders in setting you apart from being average.

4. Be a Giver
The day was a Tuesday and my phone rang. I easily recognized the name of the caller. I happily answered. The caller was obviously in a different mood than I was.

"Steve, I need to talk to you," the discouraged voice said with little emotion. Or something to that effect. It's always hard to remember the exact words when a human crisis is quickly suspected. There was sadness in his voice and I could sense there was trouble.

"I'm driving around. I had to talk with someone. So I called you"

This is the moment we prepare for. An opportunity to give to a friend and demonstrate the love for each other we often profess and too often fail to show.

"It's about Gary" he said, "The medical staff doesn't think he has but a few hours to live." Gary. Maybe the kindest and most gentle man I'd ever met. A man who convicted me just by watching him.

My introduction to Gary was a Dallas Thanksgiving one year. As we watched football that afternoon, I noticed Gary get up off the couch and walk across the room to fetch a blanket. "What the heck?" this Colorado boy thought, "It's really not very cold in here."

I was right. It wasn't cold for us, but maybe a bit uncomfortable for someone else. Gary had seen it. I hadn't. Gary grabbed the blanket, walked over to the couch, and draped it over my 87 year old grandmother who was shivering. While I was focused on the quarterback throwing touchdowns, Gary was focusing on something more important. He was thinking about the needs of others and converting those thoughts into helpful action.

Two days after I answered the phone call of despair, I awoke to this text message: "Gary died at 3:20 a.m."

Goodbye, Gary. This selfish and dog-eat-dog world needed you. But while you were here, you demonstrated, through your actions, that it's not all about us. The real champions in life are those who tend to the needs of someone else.

Thank you, my friend. Because of your example, I'll never again focus on a silly game when there are blankets nearby which need to be put to good use.

5. Become More Marketable

Recently, a well-known politician addressed the minimum wage issue. He believes that some employees aren't paid enough and that the government should mandate higher pay through law. In his comments, he said the following, "If you don't like our plans for the minimum wage, give us your ideas on how to increase people's earnings."

Okay, Mr. Politician, I will. I believe that current and future employees can do a tremendous amount in improving their value in the market place. If people aren't making enough money in their current job and desire a higher wage, instead of looking for help from the government, they can:

- Further their education

- Develop a deeper skill set

- Gain more experience in their field of expertise

- Increase their human capital

- Read more books and watch less TV

- Depend less upon others for their support

- Choose a career path which is more financially rewarding

- Produce more value for the company than they're paid, thus ensuring a profit for their employer

That's my plan, Mr. Politician. It is successful damn near every time.

6. Care for Your Parents

He is up early this morning and staring out the living room window. He quietly listens to the rain as it moistens the dry Texas ground and he draws in the deepest breath he can.

He's not sleeping well anymore. His health is telling him his last days might be upon him. Yet, health can sometimes lie. The mere presence of the people surrounding him this day though, tells him his previous days have been well spent and that, is always truthful. His wife and children care for him. They hold his hand, rub his shoulders and talk. Just like when they were all much younger. Days gone by. But days well lived.

As the rain satisfies the thirsty land, a loving family satisfies the soul of the man in need. The falling particles of moisture look into the house and can see the man quietly peering back at each drop. In better days, he immersed himself in the sweet smell of the fresh gift falling from the heavens and the gift is presented again today.

A gift not sent to ease the parched Texas soil. But a gift sent to help lift the spirits of a dying man.

7. Choices Matter
In front of you, I place a $100 bill and a $5 bill. I tell you to take either of them. No strings attached. Which will you choose?

Have you ever met anyone who would select the $5 over the $100? Neither have I. Yet, in life, it's astounding how many people choose the $5 "least valuable" option.

The man who leaves his beautiful wife and family for a low value hussy. He chose the "$5." Millions of people through the ages have let the good ones go and acquired someone of far less value. They routinely choose the $5.

Or the businessman who, out of anger, fires his top notch executive and replaces her with a lower skilled CFO who drives the company into the ground. That fit of anger just cost you a fortune, big guy! Nothing like taking the $5 over the $100.

And those who forget about and ignore their kids as they chase a workaholic career path. They gain a million dollars and lose their children. Think of it in these terms. Choosing career over family is similar to trading your luxury car for a bicycle, straight up. It's the same mentality.

Each week, we're faced with the choice. The $5 or the $100. Every person must decide which path is the most valuable to them.

Choose wisely.

8. Contentment

Someone much wiser than me once said, "Don't risk what you can't afford to lose." Following this sage advice has saved millions of people from financial ruin, poor health and lost relationships.

It's stunning to see how often people ignore this astute thinking, often playing Russian Roulette with their marriage, children, career and health. They frivolously put all of life's chips on one spin of the wheel. They risk their wonderful husband and beautiful family for a cheap office affair. He sits at a Vegas table, sure he's going to win this time and subsequently loses the down payment on the house the family is having built. Some say these people are idiots. Others say they are just not content. They are, most likely, a combination of both. Making the situation worse, they lose everything and spend the next twenty years of their life trying to regain what was lost. Ambition is one thing; foolish greediness is quite another.

Before making a questionable choice, give regard to what you need to commit to memory. Something a wise person said long before I was born…

"Don't risk what you can't afford to lose."

For the 50th year in a row, I celebrated the latest and, seemingly, monthly Hollywood awards show last night by not watching it. My level of tolerance for the Hollywood crowd wore thin decades ago. It's simple really. Not very many of them have anything I desire.

Consider what the typical celebrity has: Arrogance, drugs, booze, broken families, out-of-control children, depression, anger, jealousy, deception, hypocrisy. Yet the average citizen idolizes these people.

Too many in the elite crowd have set the bar for living really low. I want better.

Avoid the temptation of coveting what many of those people have. Seek and gain an inward sense of security. After all, if you ever receive what they possess, you may regret the day you did.

9. Create Your Advantage

A college kid told me, "No one in this country has an easier go of things than your generic white, wealthy, protestant male."

Wrong. If you want life to go well, here are some helpful hints:

- Choose successful friends – They'll challenge you and lift you higher.

- Work hard – Success isn't nine to five and it won't be given to you.

- Live healthy – In mind, body, emotions and relationships. Cast aside negativity.

- Maintain a healthy weight – It's hard to be energetic when you're out of shape and feeling fat.

- Avoid debt – Staying ahead of your finances creates confidence and a positive outlook.

- Defer gratification – Cheap things come quickly. Achieving meaningful goals takes time and is worth the payoff.

- Avoid victim status – Victimhood takes you out of the power position in your life and puts you at the mercy of others.

Like most, nothing in my life has been easy. Of the "advantages" I have, most have been acquired through my own effort and initiative. If you're feeling left out when it comes to advantage, seize the day and create some of your own!

10. Criticism Comes With Success

For decades, he was a lightning rod for criticism and insults. His joking personality, success, good things in his life, and willingness to think for himself made him a target for those eager to take a shot.

His children became fair game also. As a full scholarship athlete, his daughter was at the receiving end of rumors, criticism and hateful attacks run amuck. As for his son? Well, being a successful businessman brought death wishes, comments that his parents should have aborted him, and jokes aimed at the injuries he suffered in a near fatal accident.

Why are people at such ease in hurling insults, criticism and hate toward his family and many others world-wide? It's summed up in an old saying: "Dogs don't bark at parked cars!"

If you're moving forward with confidence and enjoying success, the dogs will bark. Dogs also sniff rear-ends but they don't create or dream. So don't be distracted by the "barking dogs" in your life. Their incessant yapping and nipping at your heels might become annoying but it cannot stop you.

Always remember. Their hate, insults and vile says a whole lot more about them than it says about you.

11. Determination
I admire golfers on the professional tour. On balance, no matter where their ball lies, they grab a club and play the shot. Whether in the bunker, in the rough, behind a tree or in the weeds, they size up the challenge and play on. No complaining. No whining of unfairness. No begging for do-overs. They play the shot.

How much could we achieve, if we took the same approach and simply played the hand we are dealt? Devoting all of our energy to the next shot in life and none into the bad luck or unfortunate circumstances which led us to our current position.

If the golf ball of your life is in the weeds today, all people want to hear from you is which "club" you are going to use to get the ball onto the green and into the cup. Quietly size up the shot and execute with your best effort to succeed.

And don't forget. Unlike amateur golf, there are no mulligans (do-overs) in life. So play on and avoid the temptation to whine and be defeatist.

12. Find Your Passion

We can learn a lot from a little six year old girl in glasses. Once she learned that she couldn't hit a baseball off of a stationary tee, she never lost confidence in her athleticism. She knew she was an athlete and simply needed to find the right fit. She tried multiple sports and enjoyed them immensely. Ultimately though, that right fit presented itself in the game of basketball where she earned a full scholarship to play in college.

Hitting a baseball off of a tee wasn't her passion nor was running up and down a soccer field hoping to score a goal. Her passion was hoops. Every moment of the day was filled with thoughts of traveling the country playing basketball in college.

So the next time you find yourself lacking achievement in an endeavor, don't toss in your chips too quickly. With a couple of alterations in your goal, you might be soaring within a short amount of time. Find your passion and excel at it.

After all, if a six year old girl can figure that out, it's nearly certain you can too.

13. Give Thanks

It's 1860 and Lake Michigan is about to swallow up the Lady Elgin and her 300 passengers. She has collided with a schooner and is sinking fast. After they jump into the freezing water, passengers hold onto any piece of wreckage they can find and hope they will survive until help arrives.

For eighteen people that night, help arrived. Help by the name of Edward Spencer, a Northwestern University student. For six hours, Spencer battled breakers and saved fatigued passengers. He swam out, tied a passenger to a rope and pulled the ailing to safety. One after the other until he was too physically exhausted to take one more trip. All told, eighteen people had been saved through his efforts. As he lay in the hospital the next day, still dejected that he couldn't save more of the stranded, he reportedly asked his brother, "Will, did I do my duty? Did I do my best?"

Years later, newspaper accounts stated that Spencer was asked what he remembered the most about that evening. His reply was sharp and convicting, "That not one of those I rescued ever came back and even said 'Thank You'"

Learn the importance of being grateful. Buy your children a box of "Thank You" cards to send when they need to thank someone. Teach them to show appreciation at an early age. Soon they will learn the character trait of showing gratitude.

In the process, they will never be the one who failed to come back and say "Thank You."

14. Goal Setting

Young people, here are a few goals which should highlight your yearly goals for decades to come. If you achieve them, your accomplishments should be plenty and your failures few.

- Each year, list five people you want in your inner circle (Read "Inner Circle Presence" in this chapter). Make sure those close to you are positive, kind, energetic and intelligent. Above all, seek honesty and truthfulness from them.

- Make a distinction between a goal and an activity. Your goals (i.e.; Make $X) should be life enhancing and challenging to reach. Activities, on the other hand, can be knocked out in a day (i.e.; Run a 10k). Maintaining a Bucket List is fine, but it doesn't replace deeper pursuits.

- Craft a list of 25 people to keep in touch with. Friends who challenge you by their behavior and will be honest in their words. If they just tell you what you want to hear, they are out.

15. Humility

After scoring a 4th quarter touchdown in the State Championship football game, the star running back non-ceremoniously handed the ball to the referee and returned to the huddle in preparation for the two-point conversion. There was no ridiculous dance and he didn't fall to his knees in self-aggrandizing prayer and most appreciated by the fans, he failed to hit his chest and point to a dearly-departed loved one watching the game from heaven.

The humble young man simply went about his business of scoring touchdowns and helping his team win without drawing unneeded attention to himself. After all, wouldn't his teammates have noticed his selfishness and formed an opinion of him as well? At a young age, he realized that success without humility tarnishes the entire event and takes away from the team. People who live for themselves for too many years will be left with one certainty at the end of their life:

They will be left with… themselves.

16. Inner Circle Presence

Develop an inner circle. This is a group of four to six people who are energetic, intelligent, wise, confident and not afraid to show strength. I have one rule for those members of my inner circle. None of them can be "Yes" people. Or "Bobbleheads" as they are called them in the corporate world. This is because people don't respect weakness or anyone who doesn't speak truth to them.

Once your list is generated, seek their company for a year and trust they will provide leadership to you and you to them. Some might make your list multiple years and some are replaced after the first year. Nonetheless, it's an effort to get better.

As stated earlier, in life, you're either getting better or you're getting worse. But you are never staying the same.

17. Life is Ebb and Flow

In your life, you will have great friends and hateful enemies. You'll have people 100% devoted to you yet will be 100% betrayed by others. You'll win championships and also finished dead last. You'll be loved by strangers and despised by family

You'll be your company's golden child and also be the lightning rod of the organization. You'll live in a beautiful house and also a ratty apartment. You'll be listened to at funerals and ignored in business meetings. The uneducated will seek your advice while the elite will arrogantly silence your voice.

So what will you learn? Simple. That you can deal with both ends of the spectrum and everything in between and that life is chock full of extremes so you better be adaptable.

18. No Whining

A reporter was interviewing an airline passenger on TV. Apparently, the passenger was on a flight in which the plane boarded and unforeseen circumstances forced the plane to sit idle on the tarmac for three hours.

The passenger was in near tears when he reported,

"We sat there for three hours with no food." Imagine that. A whole three hours without eating? How on earth did you make it? Looks like Americans aren't as tough as we used to be. One generation is storming the beaches of Normandy, knowing they're going to die, and a few decades later, people can't go a few hours without being fed.

Our toughness seems to have been replaced by whining. Always remember. The less you whine, the more respect you get, the more you are taken seriously and the more attractive you'll be to friends and strangers alike.

Many who can't go three hours without food without whining about it are unlikely to possess the charisma or stability society values in a leader.

19. Overcoming Obstacles

Obstacles. Roughly defined as something getting in the way of success. We love them and go out of our way to encounter them. Think of this. Would bowling be any fun if we knocked down every pin with each ball? Consider the act of fishing. If we caught a fish with every cast, how long would it be considered sport? Or, why do avid golfers search the toughest courses in the region?

Because they love the challenge and enjoy overcoming obstacles.

Yet when life is involved, challenges are not sought after anymore. In fact, through human nature, we tend to resist challenges and become intimidated by them. So the next time life throws a curveball and you want to bail out of the batter's box, consider the following:

From my coaching days, I remember...

- The slowest kid on one of my teams became a professional football player.

- The worst student in his class became the most famous alumni (in a positive way) ever from his high school.

- Perhaps the least coordinated runner on our team, ten years later, missed making the Olympic team by one spot.

- One athlete, who was legally blind in one, eye became one of the hottest recruits in the state and earned a full ride Division I basketball scholarship.

- The runner who finished dead last in the State Championships one year became an All-American in college and now runs professionally.

The point here isn't what these kids achieved, it's what they overcame. The fortune wasn't found in their accomplishments, it was found in the journey it took to get there. In accepting challenges and defeating them.

Look at their stories and ask, "What in my life is holding me back?" If the answer is "Nothing," then you are winning my friend!

20. Perseverance

I turned fifty not long ago. I don't know where God was in years 1-18. He seemed to withhold blessing, offer little protection and stood silently by while family and church consistently tested my inner decency and kindness.

The elimination of those influences became a springboard to a charmed life. At this stage of my life, I could never have asked for more. God's blessings have been immeasurable. Since my life really started at 19, I figure I am only 32. Had I given up at 21, my life would be drastically different today.

Perseverance. Not quitting. Learning those two traits can make the difference between a great life and one not lived at all.

Flashback: It is a warm spring evening in 1977 and I'm with a group of my school friends. While most of our peers are boozing it up or taking another hit on their bong, we are standing on a mountain overlooking the city we live in. On that night, we make a pledge to each other that, as we age, we will never quit. We will never buckle under the pressure of a self-centered society. We will never quit striving for integrity, character and decency. At the top of our lungs, we bark out, "I WILL NOT QUIT!"

Nearly 35 years later, those who didn't quit have done well. The others, who never developed perseverance, have had a tough time. One can only imagine how differently their lives might have turned out had they kept their pledge from 1977.

Screamed from the side of a mountain...I WILL NOT QUIT!

21. Pursue Excellence

As a fifth grader, she told me she wanted to be the best shooter in the state. So I gave her a simple practice routine.

Shoot 900 shots a day. She accomplished the workout daily and once simply shooting became uneventful, we upgraded the challenge to...

Make 900 shots a day. In basketball, shooters are a dime a dozen and she performed the workouts wonderfully. College basketball coaches want makers and, at the high school level, makers are a dime a dozen. College coaches want the best in the state. So we upgraded the challenge to...

Swish 900 shots a day. If it hits the rim, it doesn't count. Even if it goes in. Practice being the best. Who cares about the dime a dozen. Again, as someone once said, "Why settle for second when first is there for the taking"?

And her senior year in high school, a Denver reporter wrote of her, "Perhaps the best shooter in the state."

If you want it, go after it. And be a swisher. The world already has enough shooters and makers.

22. Speak Well of Others

I've lost too many friends. No. They didn't die. I lost them to gossip. They listened to garbage about me and I never heard from them again.

Gossips and backbiters are the scourge of society. Simply put, they are leeches slowly sucking the good out of people, destroying friendships and ruining great work and reputations everywhere. Heck, since we're calling it as it is, they are also cowards. Talking in secret and rarely giving the offended party a chance to defend themselves or present their side of a story.

If you have a gossip in your life today, get rid of them and get rid of anyone who listens to them. Both types are a negative in your life and need to go. On the flipside, make it a goal in your life to speak well of others. Doing so inspires others, creates a good reputation for yourself and attracts positive people into your life.

Speaking well of others. What's not to like!

23. Use Your Small Gifts

I spotted the trinket at a Veterans Cemetery in Arizona. In the midst of carved marble memorials and flag strewn walkways, someone had placed a handmade token of their appreciation. In comparison to the magnitude of the displays located at the cemetery, the ornament paled in comparison. In fact, some would contend it looked junky.

But for the giver, it may have been all they had to give. So they gave. In this case, what was given back through this small ornament was nowhere close to what was given on the battlefield of war. But we bring our gift anyway, showing in a small way, that those who gave their life defending our country have not been forgotten.

Even though your talent, words, gifts or skills may be small and viewed as insignificant, give anyway. Your contribution might be the very one which is needed at the time.

24. Words to Pass Along to Your Children

The whining by the younger generation is getting under the skin of the older generation. Don't get me wrong. I personally love 'em to death. They just complain too much and they feel entitled. More often than not, they think of themselves more highly than they should.

After all, ask yourself, what in life have they done? True, young people look great. Their bodies are fantastic. Sadly though, their minds don't match the level of their physical appearance. So it's often a good idea for parents to set the youngsters straight and give them a dose of harsh realities in life. So, on a monthly basis, tell your children the following:

- We will not be providing you with birth control. If you're old enough to have sex, you're old enough to finance your bedroom activities and subsequent consequences.

- We will pay you an extremely low wage for your efforts around the house. In fact, you will be paid 0% on the dollar that we make. Considering all of the benefits you get by living here (i.e. free food, no rent, free medical care, use of our car and paid for clothing), you are actually getting quite a sweet deal.

- When you are young, you will have no voting rights in our home. We'll give you a voice, but the final decision will be ours.

- You will never be promoted to any position of significance while you live under my roof. I considered a few appropriate in-house job titles for you: Chief Operating Drama Queen came to mind. As did Chief Executive Slacker. Somehow, I figured these job title promotions would only lead to more demands from them so I nixed the entire idea!

- Remember, young people. At this point in life, you have little education and even less life experience. To put it mildly, we don't find your opinion valuable when it is contrary to ours. And "No," if we can't find common ground in a dispute, we will not settle our differences through role play or interpretive dance. Those silly exercises are a by-product of people listening to others possessing a mind of mush and we're not falling for it.

25. You're Imperfect: It's OKAY to be Wrong

There is a reason that talking about religion and politics with relatives, friends and dates is not a good idea. Simply put, no one thinks they're wrong. And even if they're caught in the wrong, they'll dig in deeper and continue to defend their losing position.

Debating religion is the worst. Believers will admit they aren't 100% correct, yet they can never identify areas in which they are wrong.

Me: "It's apparent we're never going to reach agreement on this verse. I don't agree with your interpretation."

Bible Thumper: "It's not only my interpretation; it's the interpretation of spiritual people everywhere."

Me: "Well then, is your interpretation always right?"

Bible Thumper: "I would say no"

Me: "Okay. If your interpretation isn't always right, then please tell me biblical subjects in which you're wrong."

Bible Thumper: [Speechless]

Here's a solution. View debates and discussions like a tennis match. You don't have to win every point to win the match and for mercy sake, quit digging deeper when you realize you're getting whopped in the debate.

Bonus: Your Life Will Be a Mirror

Whatever you call it, what you give as a parent is what you should expect to receive once your children are grown. Give kindness; get it back. Sling crap; duck, because it's headed in your direction.

It's like a mirror twenty years in the making. One day, you look at your kids, and it's YOU staring back at yourself.

In my case, how great the pleasure was when my twenty-five year old child wrote on social media:

"Last night, as I drove to the airport, I couldn't help but remember the countless drives with my dad. Most of them were in the summer when he would wake up before sunrise to send me off to basketball tournaments. A few days later he would stay awake into all hours of the night, waiting for my plane to land and would be at the gate with a smile. He always had something for me to eat, a drink, and a pillow so I could sleep on the drive home. This level of love and support is many times thankless and forgotten. But I will never drive that long road to the airport without all of those great memories."

The good book is correct, "What you sow is what you'll reap." The universe is correct, "What goes around comes around." What you are is what you'll attract. Look at who your friends are. They are a mirror of you. Listen to how your children talk to you. They are you. Look around at your life and notice what it's made up of. Anger or kindness, success or failure, laughing or crying. That's who you are. Every time.

Bonus: Words of Wisdom During Life's Journey

- Never accept responsibility without the authority. If you are given charge of a task and are responsible for the end product, ensure you are given the proper authority to make the decisions necessary to guide that outcome. Responsibility without authority is a losing deal.

- Put a fair price on the labor you sell to your employer. Meaning, the salary you agree to work for. Don't think of yourself too highly or you won't be hired. Yet, don't think of yourself too low either or you won't be taken seriously.

- If at all possible, don't burn a bridge. You never know when a relationship or connection will be needed in the future. If you meet bad people, burn burn burn. Just be sure your decision is solid before you strike the match.

- Date and marry someone you're physically attracted to. Anyone who tells you physical looks are shallow is full of barnyard stink. Life is to be lived with passion, intensity and joy. Hard to do that when you wake up next to someone who doesn't turn your crank.

- Interact with people every day in such a way that they are pleased your paths crossed. They should be at peace and comforted that you were a part of their life, however large or brief.

Because we live in a world filled with jerks, it's not always possible. But try anyway.

- I have had plenty and I have had nothing. Take it from me, plenty is much better.

- Learn to make a decision and never look back.

- Know what you want and work tirelessly to achieve your goals.

- I once sold my coin collection so I could buy food. It would've never occurred to me to expect the government to send me a check.

- One writer in the Bible says, "I was young and now I am old, yet I have never seen God's children begging bread." Well, I have. No one, including Christians, is exempt from a growling stomach.

- Wealth is not a zero-sum game. Some people gaining more wealth does not mean that it comes at the expense of the poor. The poor can increase their wealth as well and if they do, it didn't come at the expense of their neighbors living in poverty.

- It is your decision whether you want to be rich, have your needs met, or be poor. This is a country of opportunity and individual freedom. You are at the wheel of life's car and the car will go wherever you drive it.

- Surround yourself with intelligent people. We live in a meme world. People know how to share the thoughts of others all day long. Yet they have little ability to think on their own. Much less write down their thoughts. Find intelligence and immerse yourself in it.

CHAPTER 5

PRAYER AND VENDING MACHINES

I know she meant well. But I wasn't buying what she had to sell. And what she was selling was her version of the value and benefit of prayer.

But, hells bells, she was my mom. Oops, this is a spiritual topic. No cussing if Jesus or prayer type things are being discussed. Reset. But, darn it all, she was my mom and I couldn't disagree with her. Disagree too hard anyway. I simply didn't share her views on prayer and I let her in on it.

"Why do we pray and not expect our prayers to be answered?" she asked. "After all, we put our coins into the soda machine, select our desired drink and bend over, knowing our beverage is coming." "Yet we don't do that with prayer," she continued. "We pray to God and wonder if he'll ever answer."

I couldn't take anymore and had to respond. "That's because prayer is a crap shoot, Mom."

"WHAT!," she questioned immediately. "A crap shoot?"

"Yes," I answered with attempted authority. "Because you never know what the end result of prayer will be. It's not like selecting soda. With prayer, you put your coins into the machine and aren't even guaranteed a soda in return. Much less the soda you want."

Prayer can be many things. But one thing it's not, is a two-way conversation with God. He is frustratingly silent. Nor can you ever expect you'll get what you pray for. Even though the Bible states you'll get what you pray for (Mark 11:24, John 15:7, Matthew 7:7), it doesn't always work out that way. So, what is prayer?

Prayer is often the subject of meaningless platitudes spoken without much thought behind the statement. Believers want to have faith in prayer and don't have an adequate defense when prayer remains unanswered. So they say strange things.

Case in point. There was an unemployed man. He prayed daily to find a job. Someone told him to "Pray with your feet." In other words, get off your knees and actively seek employment. Want a job? Pray with your feet.

Another man was praying daily that he be accepted into college. "Pray with your brain," a loving Christian advised. In other words, get off of your knees and use your intelligence to secure the right opportunity at the right university. Want to go to college? Pray with your brain.

All of that reasoning makes good sense. So my humorous question to you is. What would a guy pray with if he wanted a child?

Keep in mind, the Bible doesn't instruct us to pray with anything with the exception of praying with faith. The implication here is that prayer wasn't answered because the person didn't do enough. Once again, it sounds nice but it's not biblical. Another excuse for unanswered prayer is the intensity, or lack thereof, in which the prayer was offered.

"I'm praying hard for you," the social media post read. So, what's the difference between praying and praying hard? How does one pray hard? Is there a difference between soft prayers and hard prayers? Does praying hard pay bigger dividends and is it more likely to influence God into having things go our way? If it doesn't, you can always call on the Prayer Warriors of the church. Which leads to more questions than answers.

Are the prayers of a large prayer team more effective than the prayers of a 90-year-old woman praying alone without any fanfare? When did believers develop the theology that more prayers equal more success?

So why pray a prayer more than once? Isn't once all that is needed to voice your opinion/request/

plea? If you have faith, why do you need to pray for the same thing over and over and over? How about this prayer: "God, knowing that you are supreme and have no need to be bothered repeatedly, this is the only time I will come to you about this." Now that's faith! Faith that not only can move mountains but might be able to quench fires in those same mountains.

Like the fire that was burning in the Colorado mountains and was spreading rapidly. The dry conditions and hot summer sun weren't helping. The smoke rolling off of the fire caused health concerns in nearby cities. There was nothing man could do to put an end to it.

So people started praying and, eventually, left praying in secret and started going public with their prayers. Boldly proclaiming on social media, "I'm praying for rain." and "God of the ages, please send forth rain from your immense water fountains in heavenly places." So I proposed a simple three question quiz.

Question 1: Are you praying for rain to help with this and other fires? (Good, I figured you were)

Question 2: Do you walk in faith that God will answer your plea for rain? (Excellent! You pray with faith!)

Question 3: Based upon your answers to 1 & 2... Did you carry an umbrella or a rain coat to work today? (I didn't think so)

I'm still looking for just one person who prayed for rain and carried an umbrella or any rain gear with them throughout the day, knowing that rain was headed their way based on their prayers and faith.

During the seemingly, endless fire, thousands of people continued to pray for rain to help control the situation. After two weeks of reading their posts on social media and watching their interviews on TV, I offered another question: Can someone please explain why helicopters continue to deliver more water to the area than God has?

Prayer has many purposes and numerous potential outcomes. Prayer is largely unknown. But one thing is for certain. It is bound to test your faith and be careful for what you pray for, you just might get it.

Sometimes the answer of prayer leads to unintended consequences. For example, the Colorado forest fires evolving prayer had the potential to lead to an unwanted string of events:

"God, the forest fires are crazy and it is DRY! We need more rain!"

God hears their call, and sends rain. A lot of rain. After all, fires aren't doused with a sneeze. But the people aren't happy.

"God, the moisture is great but the floods are

raging, so please protect our property during the flood. We need our stuff."

So God diverts the river so the flooding won't devour their property. And, much to no one's surprise, the people kindly complain again.

"God. The river no longer flows through our town, and neighboring states no longer pay us for downstream water rights. Please help us live in a city with more wealth so we don't need money from other people"

So God, now worn-out with the whole affair, answers their request. Within days, he hears from them again.

"God, the company transferred me to Phoenix today. I promise, I'll never make demands again."

God is pleased that the people finally get it. That is until…

"God, it is hot and dry here in Phoenix. We need more rain!"

Remember though: it's not all about you. This is not your world and other people do live in it. Take a look at what people are praying for on social media: Someone in Denver needs rain for their garden while someone else in Denver needs sun and dry weather to finish a roofing job.

Three people are praying for the same marketing

job. Some snow plow drivers in Idaho are praying for snow on the roads while over-the-road truck drivers in the same state are praying for clear roads. A few investors are praying for a high market in which to sell, and newbies entering the market are praying for low price so they can buy.

So what does God do when competing interests are involved? Obviously, both prayers can't be answered to the satisfaction of those on bended knee. Keep in mind what the Bible says about prayer:

- "Therefore I tell you, whatever you ask in prayer, believe that you have received it, and it will be yours."

- "If you abide in me, and my words abide in you, ask whatever you wish, and it will be done for you."

- "Ask, and it will be given to you"

- "…so that whatever you ask the Father in my name, he may give it to you"

- "Call to me, and I will answer you…"

- "And whatever we ask we receive from him…"

- "Before they call I will answer; while they are yet speaking I will hear"

- "And whatever you ask in prayer, you will receive, if you have faith"

- "Truly, truly, I say to you, whatever you ask of the Father in my name, he will give it to you"

Setting the record straight, we get whatever we ask? Truthfully, that has not been my experience. In fact, often I've seen the reverse and I'm beginning to put it together. If I pray for black, I get white, and if I pray for yes, I receive no.

I get it already! I'm a pattern thinker and I figure it out quickly. I remember the "Can you guess the pattern" quizzes in school: 2 – 4 – 6 – 8 - ?

Or better yet:

Sunday, Monday Tuesday. Sunday, Monday, Tuesday. Sunday, ???, Tuesday.

Patterns are fairly simple and I'm seeing one here. For the past few years, whatever I prayed for, I got exactly the opposite. I prayed for a new job and lost the one I had. I prayed for a lovely lady and couldn't find one to save my life. I prayed for a house and prices in the area became unaffordable.

What I always heard about prayer from the preacher when I was growing up isn't matching with reality. "Whatever you ask in prayer, you will receive," he would read. Straight from the scriptures.

So to combat my disappointment in batting 0% in my prayer life, I've decided to pray for the opposite of what I want and need in my life.

This week's prayer list:

- Lord, please don't give me that beach front property on the French Riviera.

- God, six-pack abs would make me arrogant so please do not give to me!

- Father, please bless me with shoe size IQ.

- Lord, that lady on my dating site, you know her by her profile name, Shapely-n-Wealthy. I'm likely to lust if I date her. So please direct her to someone other than myself.

That's all ridiculous. However, praying for what I desire has not yielded the results I'm looking for. So why not try something new? After all, if a field never produces any crops, will you continue to plant there?

Honestly (and seriously) though, maybe I'm praying for the wrong things. It does happen often, I'll have you know and I'm not the guiltiest one out there. People pray for stupid stuff all the time. Consider this announcement recently posted on social media:

"ATTENTION! After a lot of thought and prayer I've decided to deactivate my website account."

Seriously? A lot of prayer over leaving social media? Someone actually tied up the Lord for a few minutes over such petty concerns? How would you like to be the angel in charge of bringing that request before the golden throne? The conversation might have looked like this:

God: "Yes, Angel Phanuel, what is it today?"
Phanuel: "I have an urgent request from Earth."
God: "Okay. A prayer was offered up that I end human suffering, put an end to disease or provide food for the starving?"
Phanuel: "No…uh…Almighty…uh…"
God: "Be bold and speak, Angel Phanuel!"
Phanuel: "Please do not smite me for this, Honored Lord, but our faithful servant on Earth is requesting your guidance on the future of his social media account. Shall he deactivate?"
God: "You're jiving me aren't you, Phanuel! Ever since we created those galaxies, you've been a clown. You slay me"
Phanuel: "Well….uh…oh forget it"

I guess prayer is not always of the Earth shattering sort. We Christians like to think our prayers are always vital. They're not. Sometimes they aren't even powerful.

The headlines read, "Christian Pastor says God told him that the United States is bankrupt and heading into economic turmoil."

The pastor needed God's voice on this? What's next? Is God going to tell this guy that Sunday church attendance will drop on Super Bowl Sunday? Or will God reveal that consuming a gallon of cold Wyoming beans will increase your chances of being bloated with gas? Tell us something we don't know.

It's amazing the things God reveals at the same time he ignores other supplications. He announces the United States will go bankrupt but remains silent as starving followers beg for food? I'm not buying it. Truth is, like the vending machine, prayer offers no guarantees. Think of the following and consider how close to reality this hypothetical report is:

BREAKING NEWS (This just in): New research findings were issued today and the results were met with disbelief across the religious world. Of note, the unemployment rate for praying Christians currently stands at 8.9%. Oddly, it's the same unemployment rate as those who don't pray. Other findings in the report revealed that home foreclosures for praying Christians up 2.7% (the same increase as for non-believers), the mortality rate for praying Christians diagnosed with ALS is 100% (the same as those who don't pray) and the average wage in the healthcare industry for praying Christians is identical to the wages of atheists in the industry.

Note: I'm seeing a pattern here. Beginning immediately, I think my prayers will be simple "forgive me" and "thank you" conversations. After all, prayer might not always be your best option if you only want something.

Say, for arguments sake, your loved one has been in an accident. His/her condition is considered life threatening. Here's the dilemma and the question of the day. You have two choices: You can pray, or you can call an ambulance. You can only choose one. As humans, we generally choose our best alternative. That's why we work where we work, live where we live, and marry who we marry. We line up with our best option.

Given those two options, I'm calling an ambulance. Most reasonable people would do the same. It's not that they lack faith. It's that they want help, NOW! Even life-long Christians know that God works in his own time and also expects us to help ourselves.

Most of us have offered prayers for years and seen no response from God. I can guarantee this. If my babies are hurt and needing help…911 it is! Then prayer. I'd rather have an occupied ambulance than an empty prayer.

Empty prayer? For example:

My friend of twenty-five years, Kyle, had been diagnosed with ALS and the effects were ravaging. His certain death was quickly foreseen and his body was visibly decaying by the day. One week he was complaining about a sore neck and only days later, he was struggling as he reached his arm out to grab a stapler.

At his last appearance to those who had been invited to a lunch in his honor, he was wheelchair bound and was rolled into the room. He sat motionless, looked around at his friends there to honor him and listened to us one by one as we gave him our warm thoughts.

Near the end of the luncheon, a religious co-worker approached Kyle and said, "I'm praying for you." Kyle looked up, glossy eyed and bewildered. He was speechless. Literally skin and bones and days from death. His strength was gone, his future already determined and unyielding. He didn't appear to be edified by the announcement of prayer being offered on his behalf. At this point, what good would a million prayers do?

When someone says you're in their prayers, are you comforted? Not if the prayer is empty.

The 100th anniversary of the sinking of the Titanic recently found the news. Memorials and prayer services were held throughout the world. Say again? Prayer services? For what? Exactly what were thousands of people praying for? That God help people in their sorrow? Are hearts still hurting 100 years later? Were people praying for God to aid the deceased in their affliction? What can God possibly do now? Were these people praying for God to unsink the sunk unsinkable?

Most likely, people were praying as a photo-op. After all, what sounds and looks better than a person, looking concerned and serious saying, "You're in my thoughts and prayers"? Didn't Jesus once say, "When you pray, go away by yourself, shut the door behind you, and pray to your Father in private"?

That instruction from the Savior has been lost in the 21st Century. Football players kneel in prayer after scoring a touchdown (but never after fumbling), politicians bow in prayer when cameras are convenient, students become public prayer warriors only after a classmate has fallen and social media is deluged with announcements of intended prayer after a national tragedy.

If you're a coffee shop customer, you're aware that they are often a hangout for Christians and Bible study regulars. It's not uncommon to see these meetings with prayer and, recently, I was treated to such a display. Here's how it went: I'm sitting at my table finishing up some items before the end of the week. Off to my left, two men are praying at the close of their meeting. One of them keeps opening his eyes during the prayer. I'm thinking, "There's no looking around in praying!"

I then break into an imaginary thought on the legality of the prayers. "Hey, Prayer Ref! Didn't you see that? Throw the Spiritual flag!" The ref saw it and throws the flag.

"Illegal use of the eyes by the man in polyester. The prayer does not count. Replay the prayer."

They continue their supplication to the Lord. And at the end of the prayer, the Praying Dude just says "Amen." WTHeck? There was no "In Jesus name" before the "Amen"? I petition the Prayer Ref again.

"Hey Ref! Unless you're deaf, you had to have heard that! You gotta make that call!" The referee didn't make the call. The potential prayer violation goes up to the booth for prayer replay review. Ten minutes later and after thirty-seven replays of the prayer, the prayer ref returns from under the hood and tells the crowd...

"Upon further review, the man leading the prayer did say, 'Amen'. However, he did not say, 'In Jesus name'. Therefore, the prayer is reversed and not granted."

The crowd boos profusely.

Okay. I embellished a bit (ya think?). But, do prayers count if you're not paying attention or if the prayer is forced? What does Jesus think about the shameless public offerings of prayer? I think we already know the answer to that one. When it comes to prayer and attempting to live a Christ-like life, I'll offer a proposal I drafted not long ago.

It was late December and I was lying around the house, footballed out and trying to utilize my brain. I was feeling like I needed to do more. In the upcoming year, I decided, I would need to pray less and do more. Too often, the needs and requests of others are met with, "I'll be praying for you." The same trite response we hear ad nauseam. Similar to, "You're in my thoughts and prayers." Long on intention and short on delivery.

People in need are begging to hear, "What can I do for you? Today."

Sweet Jean had lost everything. Her husband had unexpectedly passed away, she had lost her job, was forced to sell all of her belongings and ended up on government assistance. "At least I have my son," she said, realizing her prized jewel was still in her possession. Until he passed away within two years. Needing to turn the corner, she begged for a job. Literally begged. And her pleading brought forth vast amounts of, "I'm praying for you." Finally, Jean had enough of the empty words and replied, "I don't need any more prayers. I need a job."

Prayer is great. Immediate helpful actions are better.

If your friend needs a job, use your connections and see if you can help. If a young couple needs groceries, treat them to a trip to buy groceries. If someone is struggling in their marriage, clear time on your docket to spend time with them.

"I'll pray for you" is too often where it ends. Let's add to our prayers real action. I'm guessing our efforts won't return to us empty.

MINDLESS MINUTIA:

- Pastors have recently begun to exhort their congregation to "pray for the country." Exactly how does one do that? Who knows what is good for the nation? If a thousand people are in the pews, you might have a thousand different views on how things in this country should look. After the next election, we will end up with a zero-sum game. What some received came at the expense of what others wanted. Christians and non-believers alike.

- If I pray for my previous prayers to be answered, does that increase the probabilities?

- If I don't say Amen at the end of my prayer, was the prayer sent? Isn't Amen like hitting the send button on an e-mail? And once it's sent and we change our mind, can we retrieve it?

- "Uh God, you know that thing I said about no more beer? Uh... Where's the un-Amen button?

- Many would rather have the prayer of one person with faith and humility than the prayers of a thousand people on a "Prayer Warrior Team." People often trust the simplicity of the one.

- If all of our prayers were to be answered like we want them to be, this would be Heaven. There would be no sickness, death, financial worry, crime or inequity. We'd all be in love with the person of our dreams and have a blast every time we were together. And all 32 NFL teams would win the Super Bowl every year.

• A prayer that God can't answer? Growing up, I remember the church potlucks. Tables full of fried foods, fat filled casseroles, artery busting pies, cakes & cookies, and large amounts of soda. Before the eating commenced, a selected "man of faith" would reverently lead the flock in prayer. After much thanks, the man would pray that God "bless the food to the nourishment of our bodies."

Fat + sugar + fried + oils = Nourishment? Not even God is helping out with this one.

CHAPTER 6

HIGHER LEARNING: A CONTRADICTION OF TERMS

~~~~~~

There's no glory in aligning yourself with a bee-keeper. Just ask Hillary Clinton. Turn back the clock to 1995. In an attempt to garner more credit than what she had rightly earned at the time, Hillary announced she was named after the first man to summit Mount Everest, Sir Edmund Hillary. Hearers of the story were astonished and one helluva good Hillary story was to be told for years.

Sadly, pesky facts got in the way of the otherwise awesome story. Historians and journalists jumped on Clinton's contention and noted Hillary was born roughly six years before Sir Edmund Hillary conquered Everest. When she was born in 1947, Sir Eddie was an unknown beekeeper running around trying to avoid being stung in his wrinkled backside for the 1,158th time that month. He was a simple beekeeper. No one wanted to be him, much less name their kids after him. Until he climbed a mountain. Then he became someone and the storytelling began.

Had he retained his lowly position with irritating insects, it's doubtful Clinton would have attempted to align herself with him. After all, how many times do you hear politicians say…

"I want to thank Walter Phenargen, the inventor of kitty litter, for the influence he's had on my life"

There's no glory in beekeeping. Or kitty litter development. There is glory, however, in conquering mountain peaks, honest storytelling, and humility.

Where better to learn directness and engage in truthful discussion than on college campuses throughout the country. Right?

Wrong!

We are at a low time in our country these days as our college campuses have turned into a one-sided echo chamber. They provide safe spaces should a student be offended. Riots and shout-downs are common when speakers on the opposing side of the political aisle give their opinions. It's become a sad joke. While most college handbooks proudly announce their belief in diversity, tolerance and acceptance, the actions on the campus by students and faculty tell quite a different story.

Maybe it's time to toss the old degreed programs

into the garbage and start over. No more Golf Management, Interpretive Dance, Art History and Human Tri-Sexuality and start learning stuff which can help the student navigate life and, in the process, learn when it was people actually conquered mountains.

So, always the giver, I've decided to junk the traditional college syllabus and have explored some course offerings which actually may be beneficial for students everywhere.

Accounting and Tax Law (Pre-Req): Pay Your Own Way

Every spring, commercials sponsored by tax accountants specializing in IRS audits are heard:

"Hello, my name is Betty McIlroy and I am not an actor. I owed the IRS $1.7 million dollars in back taxes. It never occurred to me that I could go to jail. So I called Willie & Nora's Tax Relief Group. After their hard work, they reduced my IRS liability down to $5.14! Thanks Willie and Nora."

Is applause warranted for Willie & Nora? Is it commendable when tax cheats and non-filers get away with their felonious behavior and keep sticking law-abiding citizens with the tab? The shame of living off of the labor of others has become absent in America. It's become a viable business to teach citizens how to make someone else pay for the debts they've incurred.

If real learning is sought, let's encourage colleges

to teach personal financial responsibility. You incur the debt, you pay the debt. Despite what you've learned in your progressive college, the rich are already paying their fair share. Now it's time you do the same.

Business Fundamentals 101: Take the Cash

The ideas taught in this class should be so fundamental as to not be needed. Unfortunately, too many people fall for hucksters and smooth talkers and end up learning the principles outlined the hard way.

It's often called the "Help Wanted Ads" business plan. That is, a business doesn't have the funds to pay for labor, so they offer equity in the company. Future equity of course, since they currently have none. Usually, the ad is similar to this:

"We are looking for a SmartPhone programmer who can develop this really cool idea we have and make it go world-wide. We will be glad to pay you with shares in the company once this thing goes nuclear"

"Future" anything is rarely as good as today's cash. As Wimpy used to say, "I'll gladly pay you Tuesday for a hamburger today." People who haven't taken this class often fall for this non-sense. Some of the valuable responses you'll learn are:

"No. I'll give you a hamburger tomorrow if you pay me in advance today."
"Equity in the company down the road? My cur-

rent labor is worth more than your future equity." "Here's a better idea. Let's sign a financial contract today and I'll work tomorrow."

In the 1950's, employees worked for every penny they were paid. In the 2000's, the popular attitude is "something for free" and it's promoted throughout the media and on our campuses. Never forget, there is no free. It always comes at the expense of someone.

Civics 101: The Government Fails at Everything

The headline reads: "The President to launch government-backed retirement savings program."

Well, that certainly sounds impressive! Shall we expect this newbie to be more effective and more prosperous than government-backed social security, government-backed welfare programs, the government-backed War on Drugs and government-backed job creation programs?

The prize in this certified letter labeled "WIN-NER!" is this. When defining the program, the White House announced, "MyRA guarantees a decent return with no risk of losing what you put in." Sadly, that's not what I learned in Economics 101 during my college years. What I did learn was this. High risk = High upside potential. No risk = Low upside potential.

Students in the class would learn to pass on this opportunity and recognize future attempts by the government to improve their lives. Your elected politicians have driven America into debt which will never be repaid. It's doubtful they know how to make your retirement years financially secure. Welcome to a real college!

Criminal Justice 404: No Room for Political Correctness

The country was abuzz over the shootings in a Colorado theatre. What caused the tragedy, who/ what is to blame and how it can be prevented in the future were the topics of most Sunday morning cable TV shows.

Once you complete this course, you'll know that solutions won't be found. Placing ratings on video games won't prevent violence. Re-introducing prayer in schools will accomplish nothing. More stringent gun control laws will only grant more power to law-breaking thugs.

Our society is now the sum total of all of our previous decisions and choices. Whether good or bad, we are facing the consequences of our previous chosen path. We have a culture of self-gratification, a disrespectful and self-indulgent younger generation, a weak and non-accountable older population and a set of politicians with personal goals often opposite of the needs of the public at large.

Based on the magnitude of the problem, solutions aren't likely to be found anytime soon. Students enrolled will learn the concept of "$##! happens" and understand that, in a free society, things don't always go as planned.

They'll also be faced with the fact that more laws won't change anything. Future legislation will only serve to give our politicians a calculated photo-op for his/her next campaign leaflet.

Economics 101: Price vs Cost

In this class, you will learn that, while government can lower the price of something, it can rarely lower its cost. Too often, an uninformed public confuses price with cost and uses both terms like they're interchangeable. They aren't. Consider:

I'm the government and I decide that pizza should be affordable to all citizens. After all, why should only the rich enjoy pizza? Don't those with less deserve pizza too?

In an effort to right this wrong, I pass a law limiting the price of pizza to $5. "Great!!!" the masses say, "Now those greedy pizza shop owners can't unduly profit at the expense of the poor and those less fortunate can enjoy their right to eat pizza!" Everyone is excited and casts their vote for this progressive minded politician.

But understand this. While the price of the pizza changed, the cost to make it didn't. The pizza shop owner still pays the same amount for rent, utilities, supplies, insurance, salaries, equipment and taxes. Since those fairly fixed costs remained the same while the price he can charge for his product has been lowered, the pizza shop owner now can't make a profit. Within months, he goes out of business and no one can enjoy pizza. Ignorant voters are now sad and hungry because they foolishly brought this upon themselves by believing the silliness offered by the slick politician.

Remember this the next time you hear a politician proclaim that his law will reduce the price of, let's say, healthcare. The price might change for some, but the cost to others remains the same.

And the math on that one doesn't add up to success.

Ethics 100: Everyone is a Bigot

A woman is upset and last week made some disparaging remarks about those who didn't agree with one of her causes. She referred to them as "bigots." Someone subsequently asked her, "Doesn't being intolerant of the intolerant make both a bigot?"

The material presented in this class will attempt to answer that question as the pure definition of a bigot is "a person who is intolerant toward those holding different opinions."

Students will be required to outline those they are bigoted against. You don't approve of gay people? You are a bigot. You don't approve of those who don't approve of gays? You are a bigot. You are intolerant of religious people? Bigot. You are intolerant of the intolerant of religious people? Bigot. You're intolerant of the intolerance of bigots who are bigotly intolerant of bigotry? Step to the front of the class of bigoted bigots.

We are all bigoted at some level. How can it be any other way? If you have moral lines, those lines will conflict with the values of someone else and bigotry is now into play. A person who doesn't stand on any principle whatsoever, in the name of avoiding bigotry isn't to be applauded. They are still a bigot, as they have shown they are intolerant of being labeled and opposed to that opinion.

Leadership (Seminar/No Credit): Six Traits
Only students desiring greatness should take this course. Students will learn how to:

- Remove angry, bitter and negative people from their life immediately. Not this coming summer. Not next week. They will learn to remove them today. Once they're removed, you'll know not to invite them back. You'll understand that negative people drain your energy, offer nothing which will enhance your life and cause constant drama. After all, it's all they know.

- Hold yourself accountable. Nothing is more liberating than looking inward and making needed changes in your life. Quit blaming others for your failures and present situation. A huge personal growth spurt will occur once you do.

- Walk with confidence. If you're right, know it and stand behind it. Quit living in a cowardly manner. Take a stand, in kindness and with diplomacy, and don't waver in your conviction.

- Be intense about something. Anything. As long as it's productive and will pay positive dividends to yourself and others. The world has enough sluggards and too few with genuine intensity and motivation.

- See the world in terms of plenty, not lack. Prosperity, not shortage. Whatever it is you seek, there's likely enough of it to satisfy your craving and if all you see is lack, that's exactly what you'll find.

- Surround yourself with quality people. To do so, students will develop a list of 20+ people they want monthly contact with. These people are energetic, positive, fun and productive. In coaching, it's called a "deep bench." That is, a bench full of players who can be put into the game and still compete. Few teams win championships with just the starters. They need a bench.

Don't have a deep bench full of average people. Winning with average usually doesn't take place. Students will review how deep their current bench of friends and acquaintances is and make needed adjustments. A bench full of integrity, character, honesty and confidence.

Performing Arts 290: Are We Mayberry?
A look back to the Andy Griffith Show does not take many to a kinder or more simplistic time.

Mayberry actually is similar to our current society.

Notice the similarities: The jail was run by the criminals, featured a sheriff who consistently bowed to public pressure and often refused to enforce the law, employed a deputy so incompetent that his job was safe forever, was set in a town who snooped in on everyone's business and gossiped incessantly, starred a barber who couldn't see yet was granted a business license to cut hair with a razor blade, and highlighted a young student falling in love with his teacher.

Students will learn that this show for the ages was actually years ahead of its time and will be taught how to avoid being the next Barney Fife as they enter their adult years.

Political Science 100: For You, Not For Me
The old way: If your goal is to become president (a.k.a.: leader of the free world), a senator (who makes a fortune through granting favors to donors) or simply an intern (who gets all the sex from elected officials they'll ever want), you'll need to learn how to pass laws for the entire citizenry which you have no intentions of following yourself.

Take for example, the push to get better nutrition into our school lunch program. Our ever alert politicians and school administrators are working feverishly to make sure that all kiddies are ingesting only the finest of dining cuisine. Keep in mind, no law maker would ever eat those lunches themselves. Thus, the need for the course syllabus centered on real learning.

The new way: Successful completion of this course means you know how to tell others about healthy nutrition while you eat from the same menu. Remember, you'll need to remove the remnants of this morning's Twinkie for breakfast which is still present on your lips. You'll also understand the need to work out for the first time since 1978 before you attempt to criminalize the lack of physical education offerings in public schools.

People aren't stupid….oh, who are we kidding? Yes, we are. For the past hundred years our elected politicians have been passing laws on the citizenry they have no intention of obeying themselves. Colleges desiring to teach honesty and consistency will re-name this course, "Political Science 100: For You And For Me"

Political Science 370: Tell Them What They ~~Want~~ Need to Hear

Jive Talkin. It's no longer just a Bee Gee's hit. Jive talk seems to be all that we get out of Washington these days. "The economy is rebounding." "No tax increases for 97% of Americans." "This new healthcare plan is cheaper and won't limit your choices." "You're safety is our TOP priority." On and on they go. All jive.

What rational person believes anything these people say? Like the Bee Gee's sang, "You're gonna take away my energy, with all of your Jive talkin."

So what's an aspiring young politician to do?

Learn how to communicate openly without the ever so common political Jive Talk! This course will teach you how to talk less out of both sides of your mouth, make fewer promises you don't intend to keep, make believable campaign speeches and win re-election without jive talk. Once re-elected, you can thank this course that these words no longer apply to you:

Jive talkin'
You're telling me lies, yeah
Jive talkin'
You wear a disguise

Political Science 425:
Public Servants or Stars?
The annual television special showed a room full of famous actors. Dressed in glitz and smiling ear-to-ear. Crying, back slapping, and hugs all around. Each person hoping they will be seen by the American public and hoping to say something, whether true or not, that will fool the public into thinking they are viewing something special or great.

Nothing like watching the Oscars you say? NO! It was the annual State of the Union address in Washington.

During this course, participants will answer the difficult question: "Do our elected officials serve the public or serve themselves at the expense of the public?"

Political Science Post-Graduate: Politician Speak

In this class, students will learn how to give a direct answer to a direct question and avoid the all too common verbal tap dancing, avoidance, lying and deceiving. For example, these days, a typical interview with a politician looks something similar to this:

Journalist: "Senator Bonham, how would you rate your job performance in 2017?"

Senator Bonham: "When considering the economies of scale in our country, I am assured that greatness can be found in all of us."

Journalist: "Well Senator, your poll numbers are down, Why is that?"

Senator Bonham: "Please understand, John, in today's struggling economy, we need to find innovative ways to collaborate and maximize shared values."

Note the skill in which the senator slimes his way out of answering a question. This guy is Dodging The Question Hall-of-Fame material. After taking this post-grad class, the same interview will actually reflect honesty, directness and truth.

Journalist: "Well, Senator, your poll numbers are down. Why is that?"

Senator Bonham: "Well, John, my poll numbers are down because I didn't keep my campaign promises, I took bribes from foreign tycoons, and the sex-for-hire scandal I was in the middle of didn't sit well with my base."

This class is a must for everyone seeking public office or a managerial position at their local company.

Social Activism 101: Avoid Bullying Your Way to Success

The political left is up in arms after the CEO of a food company gave his opinion on a social matter. They have started a boycott and hope to either 1) put the man out of business or 2) strong-arm him until he bends his will and caves into their train of thought.

Those on the political right are also up in arms after the CEO of a coffee chain gave his opinion on a social matter. They have started a boycott and hope to either 1) put the man out of business or 2) strong-arm him until he bends his will and caves into their train of thought.

Finally! We found something we all agree on. All are in accord that if we don't get our way after realizing everyone does not agree with our point of view, we will bully them. Classic, elementary school style bullying to force others into our belief system. We attempt to take away their livelihood, shame them, harass, slander and defame. After all, the offending have committed the unforgivable crime of not agreeing with me on how things should be and my way is right, darn it! Maybe there's a more effective way to…get our way!

Goal of the Class: Learn how to gain support for your position by building a coalition. Learning to give and take. Becoming a leader after learning how to follow. Replacing double-standards with consistency in your behavior and standards.

Social Experimentation 201: Givers and Takers vs The Law of Attraction

Basically, the world is made up of small subsets of people. We have builders and those who destroy. Also present are the producers and non-contributors, the beautiful and the ugly, fat and skinny, and the two sides of any Hollywood star.

In this course, students will learn the dynamics of how opposites end up together, usually ending up in a committed relationship. Sometimes by chance in a family or co-worker environment. Other times by choice, in a marriage or business partnership.

Maybe it's nature's way of making things work. The giver pours out his/her life, finances and brain power so that the taker won't fade away into obscurity. After all, what does the taker have to give? They often offer little. That's why they're considered a taker.

The builder lays a foundation. A foundation for their family, their relationships and for a healthy society at large. It takes them years to build that which can be ruined in hours, or even minutes, by those who destroy. Often, after the destroyer has performed their deed, the builder is called upon to clean up the mess and devote massive amounts of energy to re-build what was already once in place. All because of the existence of the destroyer.

As for the producer. They are often a risk-taker who can't sit idly by when something needs to be done. They are the engine which drives job creation, contribute generously to charity, and fill untold needs throughout the community. All while the non-contributor lives yet another day void of production and never knows the difference.

Yet this is opposed to the law of attraction. Another school of though is this. If you want to know what you're really like, just look at the people that you spend time with. By and large, that's who you are. We also live in a world where like attracts like.

People also tend to attract into their life others just like them. Good or bad. As hard as it is to accept, when you see loved ones chumming with scummy people, remember, like attracts like. When the boss promotes a goofy brown-noser whose greatest talent is tattling on co-workers, always remember. Like attracts like.

How is it that misfits befriend misfits when the rest of us wouldn't even know where to look for these oddballs? How do the adulterers find those who are more than willing to commit adultery, when loyal spouses don't have a clue where even to look? What about the brown-noser at work? Who does he/she generally eat lunch with? You got it! Fellow weak-kneed brown-nosers. Like magnets, all are drawn to each other. The flipside is also true.

Good people attract the same. As do loving people. As does the boss who is qualified and has a keen sense of character in others. It's your choice. What are you attracting these days?

Your current situation is the sum total of all of your previous choices and decisions. You drove the car to your current location. Your past is the reason for your present. Success attracts success and laziness attracts poverty.

So which is it? Do you attract opposites or those just like you? This class will bring your choices to light as both viewpoints will be examined.

Transportation Engineering 345: Traffic Mirroring Life

Life is a lot like driving in traffic. At times, one slow driver has the ability to keep everyone else on the road from getting where they want to go. Likewise, why is it that our progress in life is so often made twice as difficult, simply by the presence of non-achievers?

Other drivers think that they are above the rules and put law abiding people at risk. Blowing through red lights and speeding through school zones, they appear to care not about their dangerous driving and the harm they present to others. Just like life.

People also recklessly blow through their decisions, caring only about themselves. All the while, the people they put at risk suffer and are betrayed and destroyed. All because someone believes that the rules don't apply to them.

In this course, students will learn to get some of these drivers off the road and out of their lives forever.

Conclusion

It's debatable how much value a college education provides these days. In the process of acquiring a very expensive degree, students are subjected to loads of needless information. Soft degrees are common and earned by many. All good stuff, yet not likely to give you a well-rounded education in life as you navigate through it.

Young people who successfully completed the courses outlined in this chapter will be years ahead of their counterparts as they enter the adult world.

CHAPTER 7

THOUGHTS POURED OUT OF A CAN
YOUR GUIDE TO ANSWER SILLY QUOTES,
SAYINGS AND BUMPER STICKERS

~~~~~~~~~~~~~~~~~~~~~~~~~~~~~~~~~~~

I'm driving next to the electric car as we speak and am confident the driver is a fine man. He's thin, serious looking and his hands are clutched to the wheel in the 10-2 position. He sports a salt and pepper beard, balding on top yet enough hair to ponytail it in the back. Not unlike the female in the passenger seat next to him. Also thin, serious looking, sporting a ponytail and a neatly trimmed beard.

Such is the expected look of a couple bound to have a dozen bumper stickers plastered to the back of their car. "World Peace," "No Guns for Oil," "My Kid is an Honor Student" and my favorite, "No Deodorant for Electric Car Owners."

Bumper stickers rarely account for more than "thoughts poured out of a can." In other words, trite, ill-considered and over-used beliefs generally accepted by the intellectually lazy. No one knows what they really mean, but damn they sound good! Our non-cerebral populace hears and repeats them without questioning and ultimately utters, "I don't know," when asked, "What does that even mean?"

Travel to the large conference room in corporate America for our case-in-point.

"There's no need to re-invent the wheel," the boss said. Heads around the table bobbed up and down in agreement. Who can disagree with the boss after all? If he says the wheel is fine the way it is, then take it to the bank, mister! That's why he's the boss after all. He knows more meaningless statements than anyone else in the room and his wisdom on this day is nighttime news worthy. Except for one pesky detail: Had the wheel not been re-invented, and re-invented, and re-invented again and again, our bumper sticker-filled cars would be riding on wheels chiseled from rocks. The rough ride would be enough to jar the fleas out of the beards of most electric car drivers. And her husband.

For centuries, people thought of a better wheel. Wood, stone, clay, metal. Two, three, four, five, six-spoke. Whatever the popular wheel was at the time, someone was secretly trying to re-invent it. Invention done in secret, because he didn't want the finger of wheel shame to be pointed at him. Imagine this scenario in 5 B.C.:

"Quiet, townspeople! Aquillius here thinks he can

invent a better wheel! Haha! Who can do better than this five ton wheel made of pure granite! Why, it can move a stack of bricks over a thousand cubits in less than two months! Aquillius, you fool! Don't you know there's no need to re-invent the wheel! Away with him and his silly ideas."

Even in 5 B.C., heads around the room bobbed up and down in agreement. More likely because they didn't want to lose those same heads in a noon time meeting with the guillotine had they disagreed. Supporters of Aquillius then replied with another, and still used today, thought poured out of a can response:

"Don't be so hard on him King Caesula. Don't you know that a rigid branch breaks easier than a flexible one?"

The more things change, the more they remain the same. Crap. Now I did it! Another overused saying carrying with it little impact.

Welcome to a world of Thoughts Poured Out of a Can:

John Lennon was a lucky guy. No, not because he had Yoko Ono helping out on vocals. Lennon was lucky because he lived in a world of imagination. A world of no religion, no possessions (for others, certainly not for his wealthy self) and no countries. Sadly, Lennon never imagined a world in which his idealistic followers from the 60's showered and were introduced to a razor. But I digress yet again.

Lennon was lucky. He sang, "And the world will be as one." Now, keep in mind, Lennon and his three buddies couldn't keep their rock band together and yet he imagined an entire world to be as one. He also imagined "no possessions" yet is rumored to have had a net worth of nearly a billion dollars when he died.

It all sounds good. People living as one, no one starving, everyone acting in a loving way and no one ever getting sick. But just because it sounds nice doesn't mean it's practical or even desired. Imagining all sorts of things does make for a nice t-shirt though.

But Steve, you're being really hard on John Lennon. Don't you know that "a rigid branch breaks easier than a flexible one?"

I heard that empty saying at a business meeting once and bit my tongue. You see, it was starting time and the host was on a limited time schedule. As usual, one of the regulars was tardy.

"Let's go on ahead and get started," the leader barked.

"But Maurice isn't here," said one of the team members.

"It's 10:00 and we'll need to start without Maurice," replied the leader.

"Don't be a stickler," the member said back. "Always remember that a rigid branch breaks easier than a flexible one"

Those around the table nodded in agreement. After all, isn't it better to just get along? Don't be black and white. Be like the flexible branch. Until the leader came back with, "A rigid branch might break easier than a flexible one. But which would you rather build your house out of?"

Nothing beats throwing a little truth the way of a person spewing out thoughts from a can which can't stand against the test of common sense. Later, the wise orator of non-sense discharged another gem, "Well behaved women rarely make history." She then looked around the table, gleaming as if she had uttered words worthy of national acclaim.

Keep in mind. It's important for women to achieve, thus sticking it in the ear of a male-dominated society, but as good as the intentions are behind this oft-quoted and non-sensical quote, it's important to think it through.

"Well behaved women rarely make history."

Neither do horribly behaved women. They rarely make history either. Nor do well behaved men. Neither do the rotten-behaved (That's grammatically correct. I checked.) Redheaded wiseacres in Denver rarely make history. Neither do teachers, bankers, doctors, male, female, old, young. We're pretty much an unremarkable collection of people who have no chance at rewriting the history books.

Athletes who can run fast can make history. As can rock-n-rollers who puke on stage. But people producing life-saving drugs? No history making for you! Truth is, this quote has been uttered and seen by millions, all by people not making history. But that doesn't stop people from blindly affixing the bumper sticker to their electric car and pretending they're on the verge of greatness. Maybe by eating meat and passing on the broccoli they'll make history. Otherwise, it'll be a tall order for them.

So if you think, that out of the 7,500,000,000 people on Earth, you're one of the 100 that will actually make history, then knock yourself out and post the meme.

Maybe history making will be made if people finally quit being so damn unkind to each other. After all, doesn't an "Eye for an eye make the whole world blind?"

Well, this obnoxiously painful thought poured out of a can is great in theory but poor when applied. Designed to curb retaliation after the first punch is thrown, this feel-good saying from Gandhi doesn't even pass the smell test. First off, if the whole world were blind, no one would be at a disadvantage and isn't that what liberals and socialists have wanted for decades? Equality and an even playing field? I guess Gandhi doesn't want that.

More importantly, however, is the notion that retaliation doesn't work wonders. It does!

The grade school bully in my day was Jimmy Anderson. A Barney Fife looking character who had a sailor's mouth rivaled only by the preacher's kid. Although the preacher's kid got to play doctor with the girls more often which probably incited Jimmy all the more, leading to even more harassing behavior than was typically expected from him.

These politically correct days, bullying in schools is defined as, "He called me a turd nugget." And five day suspensions are handed out.

But Jimmy was a true bully and I'd had enough the day he forcibly took my deck of cards during study hall and attempted to walk off. "No way in hell mister!" I thought. So I dropped him. Right by the pencil sharpener. His skinny backside kissing the carpet and his worn out cowboy boots pointing to the sky. And everyone saw it.

The days of Jimmy's bullying were over. No one feared him again. Nor did he test them. Years later, on the final day of class my senior year, the last person to wish me well as I left the parking lot that day was Jimmy. We had remained friends after I had delivered some street justice on his skinny cowboy backside. In this case, an "eye for an eye" didn't make the whole world blind. It did however, through force, shut down a bully. Never to return to his bullying days again.

Have you ever noticed that arguments and wars usually start long after one, or both, of the sides gave peace a chance? Not giving peace a chance doesn't start wars. Not getting your way does.

Exclusive film footage of a brawl in a foreign country was broadcast recently. No one was hurt. No blood shed and no bones broken. Why all the brawling? Because in that country, when they get mad, they take off a shoe and start beating their enemy over the head with it. It's safe to assume that not one of the combatants entered the meeting and started applying some Size 11 justice. Peace was likely tried first and peace is a wonderful goal but falls short of a solution when two sides aren't getting their way. An "eye for an eye" will never make the whole world blind. The two combatants, however, may need to take a few sick days off for a full recovery.

No one teaches peace more than religious people yet most wars over time have been started over religious beliefs. Thank God that "My boss is a Jewish carpenter"! This bumper sticker is proudly affixed to every Mom van in the church parking lot each Sunday. Right below the fish symbol. Yep, that's what Jesus is known for. His carpentry skills. I can hear it now:

"My friend, have you heard the good news of Jesus?"
"Well, yes, I have! Isn't he the one who crafted that lovely butcher block dinette set near the Dead Sea a while back?"

Just think if people made bumper stickers of their real boss:

"My boss fathered three kids from four different women."
"My boss surfs porn at work."
"My boss cheats the IRS."

If Jesus is your boss, I'm thinking his career in woodworking isn't the reason you follow him. But it's a nice skill to have when your boat is always sinking!

Those are the golden oldies and I'm proud to report, a new horde of useless sayings are being produced each year. Here's some of the latest drivel: "Young people are the solution, not the problem."

Actually, if my eyes don't betray me, it appears that young people are the problem. A quick glance through the various cable news shows and I noticed:

- Who's burning down their cities complaining about their latest injustice?

- It's not those in their 50's who are pooping on police cars protesting income inequality.

- It's young people demanding everyone else subsidize their birth control.

- From the young: Free college. I'm entitled. I want. I'm the victim. I'm not responsible.

If a person It never ends with this group. They are funny as hell, beautiful to gaze upon at the beach and creative in what they do. Being the solution to current and future problems, they are not. Yet they remain oblivious and continue to produce thoughts poured from a can bumper stickers like: "Children should be seen, and heard, and believed"

I agree…Children should be seen cleaning their rooms, doing their homework, picking up the dog poop, bringing a sibling a blanket when they're cold and practicing at any sport they want to win at.

Children should be heard saying, "Thank you," "Can I help?," "I'm sorry," "You take the last piece," and, "It's my fault. I did it!"

And Children should be believed when--and only when--- they tell the truth!

As has been the case since the beginning of time, young children are nothing special. They are naive, have no life experience, wear mismatched clothes, maintain no wealth and they usually have some type of body odor indistinguishable to those they don't know. Simply put, they closely resemble those in the Occupy Wall Street movement

Here's the bright side: It's only getting worse. Don't expect a generation of Einstein's to blossom out of the world of electronic games, smart phones, and reality television. If only they found this wise saying on someone's bumper: "The man who won't read has no advantage over the man who can't read."

Finally! A bumper sticker thought making sense. Consider. Of the written words recorded in history, how many have been read? Vast opportunities for personal growth have been set aside for activities which require no thought. Brains in our culture have been dulled into ineffectiveness. Original thought belongs to few. The most innovative thought that many people can muster up in a day is, "I'm having casserole tonight…yum, yum!"

It's a soundbite/bumper sticker/meme world. Two sentence memes have replaced reading before bed. These people vote, are raising children and are counted on to make wise choices and decisions. A wealth of knowledge is available to those who can read. Yet if they choose not to utilize that skill, they have little advantage over those who can't read. But I'd rather read nothing than ever hear someone say: "We the people."

Popular among political followers and so irrelevant as to be…irrelevant. When overinvested and powerless political junkies are upset with elected officials, they regurgitate, "We the people," like the entire country is of one accord and the same vision…

"Senator Moneybags voted **for** HB 5603. Doesn't he know that 'we the people' sent him to Washington to represent us?"

They fail to realize that had Senator Moneybags voted **against** HB 5603, others would have said,

"Senator Moneybags voted **against** HB 5603. Doesn't he know that 'we the people' sent him to Washington to represent us?"

In reality, there is no such thing as "we the people."

"We the people" are Pro-life.
"We the people" are Pro-choice.
"We the people" want small government.
"We the people" insist on government control.
"We the people" demand we go into Iraq.
"We the people" will protest a war with Iraq.
"We the people" believe in capitalism.
"We the people" have a socialist dream for America.

While appropriate when signing documents a couple of centuries ago, its usage today implies that a single goal and agreement has been reached amongst the voting public. That they stand as one. "We the people" traditionally ends when more than one person is in the room. Open minds are needed just to get along. If only the always nauseating bumper sticker, "Minds are like parachutes; they only work when they're open", was true.

Yet another layer on the nothing burger America is being fed. When you think about it, a closed parachute can be good. Like when you're carrying it to the plane. It's also good to have a closed chute while riding in the plane. It's especially good to have a closed chute when you first jump out of the plane. Or how about when it's being stored? Having a closed chute is pretty nifty when it lives in a small closet.

In a similar fashion, a closed mind can be fantastic. Most people are closed minded when it comes to child molesters. Lock 'em up with no chance of parole. No discussion and no exceptions to the rule. Case, and mind, closed. Most also value their closed mind on all things theft, abuse, murder and violence as well. How about a closed mind when women and minorities are treated shamefully? Thankfully those rascally closed minded people just aren't catching up with this open "parachute" stuff. Their closed mind has served them and others well.

Just like the parachute, there is a time for an open and time for a closed mind. Just be careful letting others dictate when you should utilize which in your life. Yet that doesn't deter non-thinkers from emitting their silliness. "It will be a great day when our schools get all the money they need and the Air Force has to hold a bake sale to buy a bomber."

It's hard to imagine so much stupidity rolled into one bumper sticker. Maybe John Lennon should have incorporated this into his aforementioned song...

Imagine there's no money
For schools nearby
No Air Force bombers

Above us only sky

First off, most schools have money. Just look at the salaries being paid to the top brass and financial shortage isn't the first issue which comes to mind. Secondly, most schools aren't holding bake sales to earn money for operating expenses. Maybe to re-supply the weekly Friday condom giveaway program, but not for teaching necessities.

Thirdly, when a foreign enemy invades our country and defense is needed, which would you rather have? An Air Force bomber flying overhead or a box of crayons and drawing paper safely stored in your neighborhood school? Happy baking. But if you need some celestial assistance with those public school issues, just remember the old meaningless bumper sticker, "Honk if you love, Jesus."

You're not seeing this canned thought as often these days. Probably because horn honking has been replaced by bird flipping and road rage. Complete with weapons of aggression. So others now arm themselves with defensive items of protection. Guns, tire irons and old ABBA soundtracks. Anything needed to scare away the bad guy.

Since when was horn honking viewed as a display of faith? After all, God knows we wouldn't want anyone to ever go out of their way and exhibit real faith! Honking is too easy. If you're a true believer, let's see some bumper stickers revealing some real signs of your faith. How about:

"Quit being an hypocrite if you love Jesus"
"Start being a good father if you love Jesus"
"Quit sponging off of others if you love Jesus"
"Get your nose out of my business if you love Jesus"

Honking is for weaklings. Actually do something if you love Jesus. To get that done, just borrow another painful bromide which is heavy in intent and light when it comes to application:"Create the World You Want to See"

Let's get this straight. The people who dreamed this up have no desire to live in the world you want to see.They want you creating the world they want to see! But since it's their thought poured out of a can, I'll play along.

Since they ask, here's the world I'll create:

- If a person wants a raise, they do something for themselves to increase their market value.

- Our children don't get a trophy unless they win at something.

- Jobs are offered to the most qualified people.

- Troublemakers are thrown out of school if they are disruptive to the learning environment of the other students.

- The money of working women isn't transferred to non-working women plopping out more babies in an effort to increase their monthly entitlement check.

- Those who burn down our neighborhoods and loot local businesses dig ditches, and fill them in again until their debt is paid in full.

- Oh. And I'll create a world in which the lower 50% of America pays their fair share in tax.

"We the People" deserve better goshdarnit! (Yep. I went there!) What's that? Not everyone likes the world I created? Well. Obviously, they need to learn to "COEXIST." Or have more "Diversity."

These two words in the bumper sticker world are perhaps the most hypocritical feel–good belief system around and usually spoken as truth by the least diverse person in the crowd and the least capable of coexisting with anyone. A person claiming tolerance, diversity, love and acceptance but quickly scorning anyone not accepting of their belief system.

It was an early spring evening in 2014 and the date began as some dates do. She arrived 30 minutes late, complained about the parking and quizzed me on my political beliefs before we were even seated at the restaurant. What? Your first dates don't begin like that?

In short order, I realized this was the date from the fiery furnace. Actually, she was a rabid activist. Same difference. For the next hour, I was treated to her views on "W" Bush, single payer healthcare, global warming and churches being tax exempt. I said little in response, thinking more along the lines of, "I know. I know. But how do you look in a mini-skirt?"

At the point she started blasting her thoughts on Civil War issues in the 1800's, I finally decided to have some fun. "Where do you get your information? Have you researched any of this?" I asked. "Because I'm not hearing very much accuracy here."

"From cable news commentators and nightly comedy shows," she replied. Whew! I was afraid she was going to say internet memes or the Telletubbies. A small smile, the length of a scar on a gnat broke onto my face. And Sargent Carter, I mean, my date, saw it! "If you laugh at one more thing I say, I'm walking out of here," she said lovingly. For me, the angels were singing, Jesus was smiling and the dead were raised. I had been set free!

"I tell you what. You use the exit door behind you and I'll use my credit card to pay the bill." Her eyes became the size of dinner plates and, for the first time all night, she was speechless. Apparently, cable news commentators and nightly comedy shows had failed to teach her anything about manners and graciousness or how to treat a decent guy. Off she drove. With her "Diversity" attitude prominently on display to anyone who would listen.

Remember, there is no "We the People," no "Diversity" and certainly no "Co-Existing." When and where did this boloney start?

Attributed to Sitting Bull, this quote confuses me: "As Individual Fingers We Can Easily Be Broken, But Together We Make a Mighty Fist"

I thought we were supposed to "Choose Peace." That we're supposed to imagine a world with everyone "living in peace." That we are supposed to cherish "Books not Bombs," consider "What Would Jesus Do?" and know that "Arms are for Hugging." But now we're treated to a lecture from Sitting Bull telling us to join forces so we can more fully kick the crap out of our adversary?

I guess, according to this bumper sticker, fists are for hugging and nothing says "Peace and Love" quicker than a clinched fist smacked in your grill by members of the neighboring community. Better than those pesky handguns. Don't you know, "Handguns kill people. They have no other purpose."

True and false. Yes, handguns kill people. Usually they are under the control of a lawbreaker killing an innocent person. That's bad. It's true as well, that they are used by law abiding people to kill savage criminal beasts who have no regard to human life. That's good.

False, however, is the assertion that handguns have no other purpose. They do, without ever being fired, create peace. Their mere presence creates a deterrent to crime. You doubt me?

Bad Guy: "Give me your wallet or I'll stab you."
You: "Let me reach into my pocket here and find my wallet. Oh, look what we have here. It's a 9mm glock and it's going to blow your manhood off in 5...4...3...2..."
Bad Guy: "Is there a store around here that I can buy a fresh pair of underwear?"

I'll make you a deal. You chase away a home intruder at one in the morning with your guitar and roach clip and I'll brandish my protective weapon. Sleep well. I'm simply letting you be you because we've been told, "There is No Alternative to Being Yourself"

I don't mind people being themselves, but it's getting more difficult by the day figuring out who "themselves" is! Let's see. His name is Paul, but he's wearing a dress. What should I do? Is he a she in which the dress is gender appropriate for she's or is he a he and not a she simply wearing a garment traditionally not worn by he's but by she's designed to look appealing to the he's?

Good grief! So I'm shopping for groceries and come over to the cheese aisle. As I arrive, an older, gray haired person with a short haircut is blocking the aisle with a motorized scooter. Still sitting on the scooter, the person is reaching, in vain, for some cream cheese. Always being the rescuer, I politely say, "Can I help you out with something, sir"? Just as I ask that, the person stands up in their scooter and the outline of large breasts is clearly revealed.

"No thank you, ma'am," she replies.

Forget living as one. Right now I'm just imagining a world in which I can tell the difference between men and women and imagining a world without Thoughts Poured From a Can. While they make good bumper stickers, they are a really crappy substitute for intelligent thinking

CHAPTER 8

JESUS: THE SANDALED SAVIOR

~~~~~~~~~~~~~~~~~~~~~~~~~~~~~~~~

I don't know much about Jesus. As children, we were taught that he loved us and we were shown paintings of him with children sitting on his knee and little lambs standing nearby. He certainly seemed like a good guy. Brilliant smile, well-groomed beard, pearly white teeth and flawless skin. Who can't like this guy?

But how much do we really know about him? Have we entrusted our entire belief system regarding Jesus based on who others say he is? Or worse, on starving artists who painted whatever was pleasing to the eye?

We were taught the Bible tells us that Jesus was "tempted as we are, yet without sin" and we believed it without question. But if memory serves, the Sandaled Savior was never presented an opportunity to view internet porn, forced to tune out a nagging wife nor given charge of kids who don't listen to a word a parent says. He did, however, face people who hated him, spit on him and put him to death. I'm thinking those trials count for far more than the temptation in viewing a pole dancer at the local strip club. Come to think of it, stealing a Christmas fruit cake might be more tempting than being a part of that crowd.

Yet the portrait of Jesus offered in the Bible isn't as clear as we were led to believe either. Consider this. How did Jesus know where the fish were in John 21 ("Throw your net on the right side of the boat and you will find some fish."), but had to ask in Matthew 15, "How many loaves do you have?." Isn't counting aboveground loaves of bread easier information to collect than knowing where schools of fish are underwater?

He knows everything about us and can recite every sin we've committed but had to ask, "What is your name?" (Luke 8), "Do you see anything?" (Mark 8), "How long has he been like this?" (Mark 9), "What do you want me to do for you?" (Matthew 20), "Who touched me?" (Luke 8), "Did others talk to you about me?" (John 18) and "Where are the nine?" (Luke 17). Jesus knows everything about every person to ever walk the earth and yet has little knowledge about such trivial things within feet of him? Maybe he was just prone to asking rhetorical questions.

Nothing about Jesus is surprising. Reading the Bible, sometimes he used some really funky and wild language. "You snakes," "You blind guides" and "You strain out a gnat and swallow a camel."

One wonders if the crowd surrounding him ever heckled him for his dated phraseology? Imagine the scene in which Jesus uttered the following: "Heareth ye my flock, you serpents, you brood of vipers...."

You can almost hear the crowd moan and finally someone whispers to Jesus, "We quit saying 'brood of vipers' back in 5 B.C., Jesus. You are SO last century!"

Haven't we all tried to fit in by talking in a groovy, happening kind of way? How do we know Jesus wasn't a nerdy guy who tried to fit in with the cool people? Yet these days, in the 21st Century, it's cool to try to fit in with Jesus. 'WWJD' (What Would Jesus Do) bracelets continue to grace our wrists, crosses are routinely seen in our homes and obituaries routinely state that a loved one went to "be with Jesus."

How do we know we even want to be with him? Granted most people want to go to Heaven, but maybe Jesus isn't such a cool guy to be with. Maybe he's not very hygienic and his nose whistles when he breathes. Or he's a mouth breather. Like guys who bowl and go to Star Wars movies dressed as their fictional heroes. Or maybe Jesus thinks he's funny by telling endless knock-knock jokes and he repeats his walking on water story ad nauseam.

"Did I ever tell you dudes about the day I walked on water? YO! Who's the man?"

"Uh, Jesus. Yes, you have. And no one says 'Who's the man' anymore."

Maybe he asks you to pull his finger. Or snores really loud and his feet smell really bad. After all, people were washing his feet for him often.

"WHOA! Jesus. Your dogs are barking, mister. Mind if we wash those things up for you?"

Maybe he's just plain annoying to be around. Forgiving, loving and your Savior. But annoying.

I really wouldn't want Jesus to live with me. Frankly, I think he'd be a bit disappointed with my lifestyle. He'd also be frustrated with my cooking, lack of weeding, juvenile joking and my deficiency in time management. Oh, and the Dallas Cowboy Cheerleader poster would probably have to go.

If we've learned anything in this life, it's that we might love someone but not possess the desire to be around them much. So if Heaven's a match for you, but Jesus isn't, it's good. Just make sure your obituary reads, "she went to Heaven but friend-zoned Jesus."

Whether or not he's a cool guy, millions of people take comfort in him. We see posters of footprints on a sandy beach and are told that they are those of Jesus, carrying us through difficult times. But if Jesus is light enough as to be able to walk on water, how come he's so heavy that he leaves footprints in the sand? Maybe it's because Jesus defies natural order. Or he gained a lot of weight after his water stroll.

Numerous times, people have claimed that Jesus alerted them to impending gloom and doom. Usually, he gives them advanced warning regarding a loved one's death or appears to them moments before their own death and destruction. Heavenly warnings before upcoming bad things is a good thing but are warnings about good things a bad thing? They must be because Jesus seems out of the loop on that one.

Wouldn't it be dandy if Jesus extended his good will and let us know, in advance, of a hot stock tip or an upcoming job opening? How about a heads up from the Messiah before our water pipes might break or maybe an advanced notice that the mother-in-law is unexpectedly stopping by tomorrow night for a visit? Where's the love, Lord???

Regardless, Jesus was a good man who taught great life lessons. That can't be disputed. He told us to pray in secret. But then the Apostle Paul told us to pray everywhere we go. I take the side of Jesus on that one. I personally am uncomfortable praying in the men's restroom. It breaks the Bro Code of chatting when answering the call of nature.

But not all of Jesus' teachings made sense. Like, "Love thy neighbor as thyself." Impossible. Truth be told, I never think about my neighbor, much less love him like I do myself. I'd hate anything bad to happen to him, but I never find myself wondering about his health or if he's eating properly. Do I think of how the economy has affected him or how his 401k is doing or whether or not his Viagra has improved his bedroom performance? I guess I can love him enough to wish him the best but anything further isn't likely to happen.

Maybe I'm not close enough to Jesus to love my neighbor as I should. I've heard a thousand times about our "walk" with Jesus. The term is used to encourage us to have a relationship with the Lord. But how do we grow in the Lord? The Pastor says we do this through a consistent walk with Jesus. "Walk with the Lord" he repeatedly says. Yet the Bible also tells us, "Do you not know that those who run in a race all run, but only one receives the prize? Run in such a way that you may win." So we walk with Jesus? We don't run? What about the races? And winning? And we achieve that by walking? The pastor later asks his congregation, "Does your daily walk with Jesus include (fill in the blank)?" What's the infatuation with walking?

As I screamed out to a tired runner once who I was coaching, "There's no walking in running!" Double-time it! Get the lead out! Hustle! Leave it all out there! No championship level coach ever encourages potential winners to walk.

Walking with the Lord doesn't appeal to me but a quicker pace is appealing to me. Because the walkers lose to the runners. Every time. Unless, of course, you're one of those goofy speed walkers. Elbows flying. Hips gyrating. Friends and family pretending not to know you.

So here's my proposal. Let's call it "speed walking with Jesus." That way, you can have your walk with the Lord and still win. But if you're going to speed walk with Jesus, just remember to keep the elbows in. And watch the gyrating hips, ladies. You don't want to lead the men into lust and sin.

Lusting and sinning. Now we're getting to the interesting stuff! Those are good things to stay away from. If your desire in life is to avoid fun that is. But lusting is usually only condemned in the context of sex. No pastor ever talks about lusting after the last piece of gourmet cheesecake at the church potluck. That's because he knows he can get the last piece of dessert and also knows that someone else will get the last piece of Brittany. That's why their lust is wrong and his isn't.

Truthfully though, the words of Jesus are solid, whether or not those who preach on Sunday understand them fully. Of the things I learned about Jesus, I appreciate most his words of "peace be still." Three words which can be used every day of our lives. For him, the words were spoken as a storm on the sea threatened to capsize the boat in which he was riding. Just three words were needed to calm the storm. The words were powerful but would have been rendered useless had they not been backed up with strength, confidence and a calm nature.

Anyone in our circle of friends can tell us things

will be okay. Voices in our lives reassuring us that things will be fine are a dime a dozen. But the commanding voice of "peace, be still" comes from a select few. It's a respected voice of reassurance, depth and maturity.

Make sure you're aligned with someone in the select few because one day the storms in your life will be crashing against you at every turn and it's not known if you'll survive one more wave. Then, the one special person in your life will come on the scene and calm the storm with a simple, "Peace, be still." Things then start getting better. It's amazing what one leader will do in our lives.

Whoever Jesus was, he was a leader. He spoke and people followed and for centuries, people have sought to follow him. Even though we really don't know much about him, we know this: the world has never seen anyone like him since he left it.

If Jesus Lived Today

I'm digging an on-line dating site because it's so simple. A picture of my prospective next wife appears and, if I like what I see, I swipe right. She is now entered into my list of possibilities. If I'm not thinking she's the one, I swipe left and she disappears forever, losing the chance to be with yours truly for decades. It's the easiest no I'll ever have. I don't have to deal with the tears and her begging for a chance at just one date. Okay, maybe a slight over exaggeration but I tend to dream.

I'm thinking the Bible and the commands of Jesus

should have the same "swipe right if you like/ swipe left if you don't like" system:

Love my nasty neighbor? **Swipe left.**
Don't look too long at a beautiful woman? **Swipe left.**
Pay taxes to Caesar? Definitely **Swipe left**!
Go to Heaven? **Swipe right.**
Go to Heaven today? **Swipe left.**
Be like Jesus? **Swipe right.**
Live in poverty like Jesus? **Swipe left.**
Give my $$$ to the TV preacher? **Swipe left.**

Using the dating site method of pick and choose, you can weed out those pesky things in the Bible which no one follows anyway with a quick swipe. Let's just be honest here; we do it all the time.

And then there's the one that always is a tweener. Stuck in between "Yes" and "No." Like the woman who is gorgeous but loves soccer. It's a tough decision. Which way do I swipe? There are tweeners in the Bible as well. Like....Be fruitful and multiply. Which way shall it go?

Be fruitful? **Swipe right**
And multiply? **Swipe left**

I've multiplied enough. And the people said, "Amen!"

Questions for Jesus
Dear Jesus,
The cheated-on wife sits in her home alone. She

is angry and bitter. Her religious friends tell her she needs to forgive her cheating husband. They state God won't give her peace until she forgives. My question is what's the timeline for forgiveness? Is it one hour after she learned of her husband's unfaithfulness? One month? One year? Ten years? Fifty years?

(Who knows the timeframe? But that lack of knowledge doesn't keep many from pointing the finger of shame and telling her she needs to do it.)

And Jesus, what about patience? Someone struggles with making a decision. They are told to wait upon the Lord. So they wait and wait. For ten years. Nothing happens. Do they keep waiting or do they take matters into their own hands?

Their religious friends tell them to take action. Ten years is too long. God demands effort. Yet if they had taken action originally, after the first three days and seen no answer to their prayer, they would have been told they didn't wait for the Lord long enough. They would have been scolded for their lack of patience and faith. So what's the timeline to forgive and to wait upon the Lord?

Thank you for your time!

Steve

MINDLESS MINUTIA ON THE LORD

• Jesus instructed us to pay our taxes without complaining yet once paid his own tax with a coin he found in the mouth of a fish. No wonder he told us not to complain about being taxed. All the Sandaled Savior had to do was a little hocus pocus and (viola!), tax paid until next time!

• All I'm saying is, if I could get a largemouth bass to cough up a few $100's, I'd be more excited about paying off Caesar myself. It kind of changes a guy's attitude on taxation when fish start coughing up money like a cat coughs up fur balls.

• I wonder if Jesus practiced walking on water first, when he was alone. Just to make sure he could do it before he tried it in front of his buddies. In coaching, you never try in a game what you haven't first successfully accomplished in practice. Maybe that's why he would go off alone so often. He was going to practice.

• And how many times did he turn water to wine while he was relaxing in the comfort of his own home? Maybe too tired after a tough day of carpentry to go out and fetch some fruit of the vine.

• I'm pretty sure that the modern-day progressive church offers strong coffee in the sanctuary to make up for the weak message from Jesus they offer.

- It's Sunday morning and I just watched a show on cable TV, "Sex in the Days of Jesus." Does watching this program count as going to church?

- How many of our long lost relatives actually aren't in the loving arms of Jesus like you thought they were? Imagine the day you arrive in Heaven and you look around for them and are told, "No, your Aunt Donna, brother Rico and Grandfather Pappy aren't here and they never have been. They all went to hell. Sorry."

- I wonder if God and Jesus play jokes on us.

In Heaven one day, you'll ask God, "Lord, why did you put me with that dastardly husband of mine for 64 years?" and he'll reply,

"Hey, it was a joke. When Jesus and I came up with the idea and put him at that college party you attended, we thought you'd slap him across the face and we'd all have a good chuckle. We had no clue you'd fall in love and marry him! I mean, he was a lying, cheating drunk for crying out loud! My bad."

- Is it possible to, once you get to Heaven, actually get thrown out? That your behavior is so poor, that God gets the Heavenly bouncers and performs some street justice on your wayward backside? This is a real possibility for some people I know.

• And after all, it's already happened once! Just ask Satan.

• What if I don't want to sing for eternity? Do I have to? The thought of it sounds really boring to me.

• "No, God, I won't be singing for the next 5 billion years. The same songs over and over. And, by the way, after being up here for 946 million years, Peter playing the air guitar during worship isn't funny anymore. Just thought I'd pass that along"

• What if Jesus feels so awkward around the ladies that he tries too hard to impress them and forgets to hold the golden gate open for them when they arrive? After all, he did spend his life roaming around with just guys.

• I wonder why Jesus chose carpentry as his career. Did he have a passion for it? If he was asked that question, would his reply be...

"I have no passion for carpentry. But heck, it pays the bills until something else better comes along. Or until a fish coughs up more dough!"

CHAPTER 9

PEOPLE, DOGS AND THANKSGIVING MEALS (THE AMAZING DYNAMIC OF CROSSING PATHS)

~~~~~~~~~~~~~~~~~~~~~

Tumbleweeds are nervous when they blow through this side of town. Not because they fear for their vegetative life, but because they may lose their love of it just by rolling past. Violent crime here is not the issue; poverty and lack of social graces are the concern. Lack in financial standing among the local residents has produced anger, ill-health and discouragement.

The last time I visited this harsh area, I had shuffled past five obviously homeless men congregating on the sidewalk. Having completed my business for the day, I was focused on finding my car and scurrying home. The surroundings I found myself in didn't fit me well.

"Hey, Hollywood. Nice suit!" one of them yelled as I passed by. I quietly considered his comment and withheld any amusement I found in his description of my appearance.

True, it was a blazer with designer blue jeans yet hardly a suit and quite distanced from anything you'd see reflected within the affluence of Tinseltown. Nevertheless, the brief discourse had reinforced something I'd known for years. One man's downtown Denver is another man's Hollywood or, as I would learn in the immediate future, one person's worst-case scenario is another's stark reality.

Random acts of unpleasantness display their ugly head in this 'hood far more often than random acts of kindness and I returned to the area a few weeks later on Thanksgiving Day with the purpose of handing out holiday meals to people in need. A dilapidated motel, not far from where I had encountered the homeless men, was the target area for the food giveaway. Mind you, I was not delivering invitations to people needing a place to go for Thanksgiving dinner. My friends and I were bringing food to people in need. This is the place where the equation is simple:

No food delivered today = No one eats today.

Within the borders of the motel, I heard about a family of five with another child on the way. Their apartment was nestled on the first floor, behind a heavily dented front door and feet from the parking lot littered with broken bottles and common trash. The stains of vomit and drunkenness were apparent throughout the entire complex. The smell of cigarette smoke and various other substances were not difficult to detect.

Hollywood this was not.

The family was squished inside their one-room hotel/apartment/home and, as we approached the door, I spotted a small redhead girl standing by the window, peering through the tattered and soiled curtains. She couldn't have been more than two years old. She saw me and I made eyes at her, smiled and waved. She offered a smile in return.

I knocked on the door a couple of times and the mother of the children was quick to answer. She looked at the three strangers standing quietly at the entrance and beamed. Spying several boxes of food in our arms, she had figured it out quickly. Her hungry family would be the recipient of Thanksgiving dinner on this day.

As the adults exchanged pleasantries, the little girl caught a glimpse of me standing at the door, left her perch on the window sill and walked toward me. Obviously, something she desired had caught her fancy. Within seconds, she had arrived at my feet, extending her arms. She wanted a hug.

In a world of billion dollar profits, million dollar salaries, self-driven cars and living with someone else's heart, she was requesting one of the simplest gifts known to man. Human touch. I was the giver, she the taker. Or so I thought until it occurred to me: Is receiving a hug what she wanted at all? I had simply assumed I knew her intentions.

What if she wanted to be the giver and leave me with a cherished gift? Maybe she saw, in the pain on my face, that this was my first holiday after the horrible end of my thirty year marriage. Did she pick up on my countenance that I had no home for Thanksgiving myself? That, for the first time in three decades, either I'd be invited to someone else's home for Thanksgiving or I'd celebrate it alone? What was it those little eyes were seeing and what was the mission of those adorably small arms?

I looked down, and seeing a mountain of human kindness packed inside a 36" tall body, bent over and hugged her. All the while, those standing at the door were witnessing the kindness the old guy is giving the young girl. They couldn't have been more mistaken.

In quick fashion, she had become the giver and I the recipient of the most loving and rewarding gift I'd obtained in a thousand nights. If the homeless men in the area wanted Hollywood, they wouldn't discover it in her either. For inside her simple act of kindness was found no acting, pretense or arrogance. Just her as who she was. A young giver showing the older generation the definition of kindheartedness.

The Bible says, "Some even entertain angels unaware." The media will label those who provide, cook or deliver Thanksgiving meals as angels.

Many, however, will say the angels in this story were the homeless men who piqued my curiosity, prompting my return visit a few weeks later. Others would say the angel was the mother of the children who graciously, and humbly, answered the door with three uninvited strangers standing there. My vote, however, goes to the smallest person in the story.

The two-year old redhead will never remember me yet I will never forget her. What a treasure I found when my friends and I searched for people in need of a meal. For within the vomit-blemished sidewalks of a dilapidated hotel complex, I found a beautiful and loving two year old heart which gave more to me than I can ever give her and, in the process, had entertained an angel unaware.

Consider the people we meet in the course of an average week, much less than in an average lifetime. Some we'll grow to love, others we'll grow to dislike. Most will remain neutral in our lives. But all will be someone who passed through our short span on this earth and the impact they make in our lives will be a smorgasbord of contrast.

Just days before I met the little girl, I had come home to a handwritten note. It was from one of the most recognized names in America. The note was sitting in a frame on my kitchen table and was the result of a meeting between him and a dear friend of mine. In the course of the conversation, this man, one of the busiest and in-demand men in the country picked up a pen and scribbled out a note of encouragement to me. The note was short and to the point. He simply wanted to reach out and say thanks.

This guy gets it. The power of a compliment and what can be accomplished in one minute. Human beings are hurting and in need of inspiration and reassurance. Like this man, people builders are out there and are more needed than ever. They enter our lives one minute and are gone the next. Yet what they leave behind will be remembered forever.

The people we encounter in our lives. Some, like the little girl, are givers even when they have no understanding. Others, like the man who scribbled the note, make a point to leave their positive energy to every person they encounter.

People. Easy to hate at times and 100% fascination other times. So many differences yet we're basically the same. People. So unlikable yet so lovable.

Think of this: Four. A small number when compared to the seventy-five thousand people I've encountered in my fifty years. In the numeric world, that's 4 out of 75,000. Four what?

I wish only four people had never entered my life. These four caused me so much pain, discouragement and sadness that I rue the day that our paths met. When viewing it through that lens, life is pretty good. That means, of the people I've encountered in my life, 74,996 of the 75,000 didn't really cause me much harm. Those are pretty good odds.

Generally, I love people, even when I meet some-one new and realize the connection just isn't there. They leave you with two choices: 1) be rude and come across like a jerk or 2) have fun with it.

I choose to have fun with it.

One summer, I was suffering from a running injury which required that I become a cyclist. Not a skin-tight, spandex-wearing, showing-every-nook-and-cranny-of-my-manhood kind of cyclist. But a ride-just-to-burn-calories kind of cyclist.

So I took the plunge and made some upgrades to my bike. To do so, I made a trip to my friendly local bike store. Little did I know:

Me: "Hi. Do you have bicycle seats here?"
Salesman: "No."
Me: "But it's a bicycle store."
Salesman: "They're not called seats. They're called saddles. We have saddles."

(Good grief. I'm not sure I can handle this guy. Now it's decision time on my part. Be a jerk or have fun.)

Me: "Saddles? Well howdy doody then, partner! While yer a fetchen me a saddle, I'll just mosey down to the lower forty and scare me up some grub."

Salesman: "Are you for real?"

That's what you get when you choose fun. If you don't see the humor in all of this, life's ride will be a rough one and, chances are, you'll end up with far more than four people you wish you'd never met. As someone once said. "Love your enemies because you're the one who made them." True enough. You do have some control over your enemy count.

If you choose the go-along-to-get-along route, do know that making it fun will be an excursion for a lifetime. The comedy will never cease while, at the same time, your frustration level with people will wane. Try it.

Aly: "Dad. I want to buy you an ice cream shake. Just pull through the drive through"

We pull into the local ice cream joint and come to a stop at the ever effective ordering Speaker.

Employee (On the 1961 technology speaker): "Wjend akkas vat bluffaque mimmortakaelt?"

Translated, "Welcome. May I take your order?"

Me: "Sure. We'll have a small Chocolate/Peanut Butter Burst and a large Carmel Boomer"
Employee: "Okay. That's a small Chocolate/Peanut Butter Burst, one large Chocolate/Peanut Butter Burst and one large Carmel Boomer?"
Me: "No. One small Chocolate/Peanut Butter

Burst and a large Carmel Boomer"

Employee: "That's a two small Chocolate/Peanut Butter Bursts and a large Carmel Boomer?"

Me: "No. ONE small Chocolate/Peanut Butter Burst and ONE large Carmel Boomer. Please read that back to me"

Employee (In a super condescending tone): "That's oneeeeeee smaaaaaaall Chocolate/Peanut Butter Burst and oneeeee larrrrrrrge Carmel Boomer"

Me: "You got it"

After a short wait in line and a few laughs regarding the obvious difficulty of our order, we pulled up to the window and received our tasty treats, took one bite and realized….The employee had given us one small Carmel Boomer and one large Chocolate/Peanut Butter Burst!

Be a jerk or have fun with it. End life with four enemies out of seventy-five thousand when you could have chosen the ton-of-enemies path. You'll live longer by making the right choice and it'll be a daily affair until the day life ends.

Think of the frustrations in an average day. From the moment the alarm sounds you'll be tested. Let's go through a few challenges together:

It's a New Day
It's 5:00 a.m. in Steve' neighborhood and you know what that means. It's time for the daily, "Who can make the most noise and wake up the neighborhood before the sun rises derby!"

The horn sounds and they're off!!!

The contingency of barking dogs get out of the gate quickly and with full gusto. The dogs believe that their purpose in life is to bark it up all day while driving down property values. That's right. They know real estate trends and will do whatever is necessary to make homes affordable to all. At least that's what appears to be the case.

Hot on their heels this morning is the firing up of diesel engines and needless idling of gas guzzling, fifty-ton trucks throughout the neighborhood.

And the competitors round the first corner in this exciting Derby of the Noise!

Don't look now, but making a serious charge to win today's noisiest creature alive derby is a newly purchased Harley ridden by Billy Bob Rondell, a fella who thinks buying loud things makes him a good neighbor. Just ask all nine of his shoeless children. This is exciting folks! It looks like a race to the finish. The noise is tremendous and the annoyance level of the participants is at an all-time high! Your good nature is being tested and you're not even out of bed yet! And the winner by a decibel...is ...the neighbors broken sprinkler head as it sprays a fountain of uncontrolled water upon the roof of their 1996 Honda! Tune in tomorrow and see if the daily cat fight will return to its normal place in the winner's circle!

Such is a Day/Week in the Life of the average American. Life is great and so is our country. Yet living a day in it presents challenges, laughs and opportunities like none before.

I wondered, at 5:00 this morning, if I can control my frustration with the neighborhood noise by looking at it a different way? Why is the dog barking so exasperating while the bird chirping is soothing and almost therapeutic. Both creatures are just doing what they naturally do, just like humans. Maybe this 5:00 a.m. challenge is just a warm-up to what I'll encounter later in the day.

Like the dog and the bird, some people jabbering non-stop drives many folks crazy while the voice of others brings comfort to the hearers. As I attempt to navigate through this day, I'm resolved to listen to more human birds and clear my soul from the dogs who bark all day.

But, before the birds in my life get arrogant hearing my resolve, just remember. Nobody protects their house or property with a bird. When it comes to toughness, people want a dog. There you have it. It just goes to show that both birds and dogs, literally and figuratively, have something to offer.

Whether they're annoying or not, take heed. No two days are ever alike. Each day, you'll encounter people you'll never see again and maybe do things you'll never be able to do again. No one has ever disputed the variety of life.

Recently, I had the experience of being in the same room with a United States Senator and a Presidential candidate. In contrast, just a few days before, I shared a meeting table with people who discussed, during a staff meeting, their favorite cartoon character growing up. That's a contrast of two different worlds brought forth by vastly different people. Spending time with cartooners one day and with those on the world stage the next. There will always be variety in the people you cross paths with daily. That's a guarantee.

This level of diversity, combined with fantastic air travel options, also enables us to eat breakfast in New York City and lunch in Los Angeles, encountering every lifeform in between. How many friendships had their beginnings at an altitude of 35,000 feet? I can think of at least one:

I noticed him the second I stepped onto the plane. A young man in his mid-20's, long hair and with sharp features. It was obvious he was an athlete. My intuition told me immediately he was a talker and I wanted to avoid him. I was tired and wanted a simple plane trip with no effort involved. "I don't have the energy for Fabio over there," I thought. Please don't let my seat be next to his.

I guess I didn't want a repeat of a flight earlier in the year in which a passenger whipped out a homemade tuna sandwich for her on-flight dining experience. Some people simply don't get it. I didn't know anything about this guy except I hoped my seat was elsewhere and that he didn't bring odiferous fish onto the plane. Yet fate had other ideas. As I looked at my ticket and gazed at the seating displays by the overhead bins, I soon learned my window seat was smack dab next to his center seat. Karma had reared its ugly head and I feared it would be a long flight.

"Hey man," he said as I sat down.

"How's it going?" was all I could muster up. After a minute or two, I cut to the chase. You see, if I'm going to engage you, I go for the kill. I'm all in. I want to know your story. What it is that makes you tick. Within five minutes, he's singing like a bird and telling me about his life in full.

Who he is, is one of the fastest sprinters in the world and he has a scrapbook as thick as the concrete walls at a nuclear waste site. I know that to be true, because I researched him on the internet when he wasn't looking. Simply put, this man was a beast! He told me about his days at a college track powerhouse, about destroying the entire field in the state championships in high school and how he ended up on the wrong side of track snobs everywhere.

During our conversation, I found him to be one of the brightest young men I'd ever encountered. Simply put, he got it more clearly than most CEO's in the country. He offered leadership, clarity and a bright outlook which surpassed anything I get from most people my age. All despite the fact people all over this country choose not to support him.

The flight ended and I realized it was the shortest flight I'd ever encountered. All due to a long haired world class athlete who can flat out pick 'em up and lay 'em down and impress an old guy who just wanted to sleep. It's about listening to the birds and turning a deaf ear to the dogs. It's an attitude.

People are amazing. Some are born with the proverbial silver spoon and seemingly breeze through life while others can take something small and use it to a positive advantage. Like the guy who drove a small compact car. While he was well-liked, he was no ladies' man by any stretch of the imagination. Primarily because he drove a compact car. If only they hadn't judged him so quickly.

It was a perfect car for him, decent to look at and ran like a well-made watch. The problem was, he needed to upgrade for business purposes. He was reluctant to part with it for reasons known only to him. After all, while owned by him, the car had delivered a trunk full of food/clothes to several families desperately needing them, drove sick people to the doctor and picked up others from the hospital. It was used to drive a girl to basketball practice because her mother was too sick from radiation to do so. It had taken kids to college and also heard conversations of a life changing nature which were held within its friendly confines. The car had also driven to the bank often and retrieved money for purposes higher than saving for retirement. His trusty mechanical friend had enabled him to meet with those he loved and drive away from spirit-killing situations. The list went on.

When I view local parking lots full of luxury vehicles, I know that his car was never the most expensive car to be seen. But when I considered what was accomplished with his car, I realized that he might have owned the most valuable car around.

On one end of the extreme, you encounter the giver--the guy with the car. At the other end of the spectrum are the people who have nothing to give and you'll encounter both during the course of a week. Birds and dogs and the ability to listen to either. Again, choose wisely.

As part of his job, my son and I were out filming some on-the-street interviews when we stumbled across a homeless man. Actually, we stumbled over the homeless man, as he had a bunch of stuff strewn over the sidewalk, but that's a different story. We had our camera in tow and approached the man to get his thoughts on the recent election. Upon hearing our request, the man gave us some attitude and announced that we could interview him. For $30.

What an interesting study in human nature. This man will consent to a three minute interview for $30. Extending that pay rate, it equates to $600 per hour! While I'm not an economist, nor have I ever performed a pay study for certain professions, I'm thinking he's overvalued the worth of his opinions. My hunch and my gut feeling is that this guy's market value does not exceed that of the top attorney's in the area.

People are an interesting lot to be sure. Just when I think I'm onto them, I get thrown a curveball at a hundred miles per hour. With roughly eight billion people on earth, how do we end up with such a small fraction of them becoming enemies?

Not long ago, I attended the viewing of Lincoln, the movie. (I'm trying to make this sound more important than what it was.) I hate to spoil it for you, but at the end of the movie, Lincoln gets shot and he dies. It was horrible and sad.

Near the end of the movie, a 23-year-old woman sitting behind me started sobbing like a baby when, in the film, some guy announced, "the president has been shot." Maybe this news caught the young woman by surprise. Or maybe it's simply still too soon. Whatever I do, I will never go to Titanic with this woman!

Crying over something which happened one-hundred and fifty years ago? Probably not normal, yet real just the same. People are all different. They can make your day or ruin it. Largely, it's up to you which will occur.

Birds and dogs. There's always room for both in your life.

CHAPTER 10

"YOU DON'T WANT TO KNOW THE FUTURE" FOREGOING THE CRYSTAL BALL: DEATH

She had been on life-support for two days and her family pondered their next move. Her body wanted to die but her family didn't share that view.

"She has a zero percent chance of survival," the attending physician informed her husband. "What would you like us to do?" After a few moments, the husband replied, "Keep her alive for another day." Those nearby wondered. With a zero percent chance of survival, what's the purpose in prolonging the inevitable? Maybe the man heard the "percent chance" and not the "zero" or maybe he subscribed to the thought, "Everyone wants to go to Heaven, but no one wants to go today." Regardless, for whatever the reasoning, death was postponed and, seemingly, feared.

Ecclesiastes (7:1) tells us the day of death is better than the day of birth. Maybe for the person dying but certainly not for those who grieve. I once had a neighbor who didn't believe in physical fitness or eating well. Basically, he was committing suicide on the installment plan. Dying in small doses. One day, he received a scare via his complaining heart and it alarmed him. As could be expected, he made a deal with the Lord and turned over a new fig leaf.

"I don't know when I'll die," he said, "but I just want to live as long as I possibly can."

"Not me," I countered. "I don't want to die today or outlive my good health. So death anytime between now and then is when I want to go." Why would I want to outlive my usefulness or ability to enjoy health and peace? When I'm ninety and sick, please don't send the prayer warrior team to pray for my healing. And don't write a five-hundred word obituary outlining my every achievement. And, for the love of Pete, don't cry and wail at my funeral.

My life was wonderful. I had two of the greatest children I could have ever asked for. Exceptional health, fantastic friends, a million laughs and I dated beautiful women. I was never hungry or without shelter and I had the pleasure of meeting awesome people from every part of the world.

There comes a time in life, in which it's time to go. Meet some people whose time came.

Living a Life With No Regret: (Greg)
"Oh no, Steve!" he said as he looked down at his

plate. "You do not want to know the future." He shook his head, looked away and became silent. It was Christmas of 2001 and I was sitting across the table from my older brother Greg. I had just commented on how valuable a crystal ball would be in life. We had often discussed issues which carved across a broad spectrum of topics. Wouldn't it be great to know the future? On this night however, my comment obviously struck a concerned nerve with him.

Traditionally, our family Christmas dinners had been filled with laughs, good food and a house full of children still being raised. This night was not different. With one exception, however. To me, Greg seemed troubled. As he would comment a few days later, "I had the eerie feeling this was our last Christmas together." Little did we know at the time how right he was and how blessed we were that we had lived a life of no regret with Greg. And that he had lived the same way.

The annual family Christmas party began. A hundred presents under the tree, food in abundance on the table and a pleasant vibe from those in the room. Greg's comment, a few hours later, still had not resonated with me. But why would it? The family party had taken its usual turn. Much to the amusement of our mother, Greg and I horsed around right before dinner. "You boys are so funny" she commented. Our small children opened their packages, Greg and I tried to pull down the trousers on SpongeBob Squarepants, people waited eagerly to see who would get the annual prank gift (the dreaded corn stalk casserole bowl) and sidebar conversations often took hold.

As usual, it was a fun evening and the five hours which had passed seemed like thirty minutes. The excitement gave way to fatigue and the house began to clear out. As I began to drive away, I told my wife, "Oh. I didn't tell Greg goodbye. I need to go back in." and, in a moment I've thought about a thousand times since, she replied, "It's okay. I wished him Merry Christmas and said goodbye for us."

With that, I drove away from Greg until eternity. Carrying with me the roll of film I had in my camera that night. Film which would be developed within a couple of weeks and by the time I picked it up from the developer, life had changed for everyone in the picture. With the words Greg had prophetically offered at dinner, "You don't want to know the future."

The family Christmas gave way to New Years and the hope of decent weather until spring could arrive. "Ah, it's nice to hear her again," I thought as I headed out of the house to grab some coffee. It was my daily ritual and had been for years. Leave the house before the kids wake up, have some time alone and get ready for the day and on this dark, January morning in 2002, the bird was as noisy as ever.

I had missed Lady Chatterbox. It had been a couple of months since she had graced us with her non-stop jabbering from a nearby tree. She was a welcomed addition to this winter morning. A Colorado warm front had also blown in overnight and I stood on my driveway, taking pleasure in the soothing wind. I was confident my five mile run later that day could be accomplished in shorts.

The dark, warm and quiet morning (Lady Chatter-box withstanding) gave way to a busy day and my fatherly duties pressed for my attention. Gotta get Caleb, I kept thinking. I can't forget. By mid-af-ternoon, I was sailing down a Fort Collins road to get my son. Sailing that is, until I encountered a stream of emergency vehicles and rescue person-nel headed down the same road. I pulled over and allowed the caravan of sirens and noise to pass by.

"What the heck is going on?" I wondered. It was unusual to see such a large convoy of vehicles rushing to an emergency and I gave it no further thought. Within a couple of hours, however, I would gain more understanding of the commo-tion I had encountered. Starting with the voiceless and rhythmic blinking red light on the answer-ing machine upon my return home. No messages left. Just hang up after hang up after hang up. So I went about my business. The red light contin-ued to blink. Saying nothing. But trying so hard to communicate with me.

After a long day of traversing the town, we were finally home and like flooding water in search of any path it can take, the phone rang again. It was pursuing me. Relentlessly. Fifteen-year-old Caleb answered the call and brought me the phone. "Dad, it's someone named Larry Baker. He wants to talk with you."

I knew, whatever it was, it wasn't good. There was no reason this man would ever call me unless it was bad. I just knew. "Steve," said the voice on the other side of the call, "It's your brother Greg. He was in an accident this afternoon and he didn't make it." Confused, I asked him to repeat what he had just said. So he did and with that, my ridiculously charmed and innocent life came to an end. It was over.

But it was over with no regret. For Greg and I had known each other for forty-one years. In that time, we had packed eighty years of life into each other. A million laughs and a million thrown footballs. Staying up at night when we were boys, seeing who could fabricate the coolest story. Sneaking into the drive-in R rated movie hoping to catch a glimpse of a scantily clad female. Marbles, sunburns, cruising for chicks all night, model rockets. Igniting firecrackers that could blow your hand off. Baseball cards. Lighting a lake on fire. Countless hours fishing, playing basketball, riding bicycles. Tubing down a flowing irrigation ditch. (Not knowing how to swim was just a minor detail.) The Dallas Cowboys.

No regrets.

Someone once said, "Sometimes God gives you a tornado to prepare you for the hurricane."

Was Greg's death the tornado? Or a vision of an oncoming and unseen life hurricane? To answer that, I'd need to review my life since Greg's death. It hasn't been easy so I have no answer for that. All I know is that he was gone too quickly and I never had any input on the situation.

His death was sudden and random. All it took was a minor loss of control and his new car was upside down in an irrigation ditch. And he was unconscious through it all. When he was finally pulled from the icy water, all that remained was a faint pulse. A pulse which was soon lost as well.

I still visit the gravesite every so often. I've been there when it was ten below zero, during a driving rainstorm, in the blistering summer heat and at midnight, when I wasn't supposed to be anywhere near the cemetery. I have no illusions that Greg hears me when I speak to him. But it's kind of therapeutic to chat with him at the site anyway. Just saying hello or letting him know that I'm still jogging the same five mile routes we marked out together thirty years ago. Sometimes, I've given him an update on my kids. But I never update him on the Broncos. Or politics. Only on stuff that matters. I look at his tombstone. A depiction of where he caught his first fish in the canyon he loved so much. I stare at the little fisherman engraved in the stone. Look for it. It's him. Complete with his fishing rod.

Time marches on and so do I. Filling my life with good people and healthy life choices. Getting rid of weights tying me down and striving to take advantage of every talent I might possess. In other words, living life with no regret.

Because, according to Greg in our last minutes together, none of us know what the future might bring.

Valuable Lunches at Little Cost: (Matt)

We were in junior high and ate lunch together every day. My brother Greg, myself...and Matt.

Funny, the things you remember about someone. All three of us had a dry sense of humor, loved the Dallas Cowboys and enjoyed playing basketball when lunch was finished. Even though forty years have passed since we walked those halls, I remember the laughs and even where our table was in the cafeteria.

It's not a surprise we three got along so well. The traits we exhibited at an early age became full grown in our adult years. We ended up with solid careers, beautiful families and became productive community members. Yet the sand in the hourglass of life flowed quickly and death raised its unbiased and unforgiving hand again. For not long after we lost Greg too soon, Matt too was killed in an auto accident.

To grieve is expected and necessary. But rejoicing can also have a healing place in the process as well. I rejoice that three young kids shared a lunch table four decades ago and that our lunches didn't simply consist of nourishment packed inside our lunchbox. It was nourishment leading to the ultimate building of strong men and I rejoice that we made each other better, even though that was never our purpose.

Long after we left the junior high cafeteria, we grew into men, raised our families and lived our lives. But for a brief moment in time, we sat at a lunch table and dribbled basketballs on the playground. The same sun which warmed us then warms me now. We move on but the sun remains the same, showing me how insignificant we are. What's not insignificant, however, is the time we invested into each other and the bond we developed. Unknown to us, we became a small part of each other's short existence on earth. We shared our food, conversation, rotten jokes and we shared in life. Two lives of which, have now ended.

So congratulations, gentlemen. You lived life well. You were great fathers and devoted husbands. I might see you soon. Who knows? Until then, I'll remember our bologna sandwiches and asking each other every day, "What's in your lunch?"

Invaluable stuff at little cost, that's what!

Leaving in Separate Directions: (Dee)

She was beautiful and I was funny. The mix of the two encouraged something I always told my son as he grew up. "Few things in life match the awesome sight of making a beautiful woman laugh." When a beautiful woman laughs, her already glorious face takes on a new look. Her game is raised to the next level and having the ability to make her laugh is a gift not everyone has the pleasure of experiencing.

"Steve! Stop! Your jokes are so bad!" The gorgeous, barely thirty years old, mother of three told me as she walked away. I had just busted her up with a wisecrack of mine. In hindsight, it was probably not that funny, but it did bring a smile to her already lovely face. I watched her walk down the hallway, still chuckling at the joke which I remember to this day. Then, I retreated in the opposite direction and went about my day as well.

The Bible says our life is but a vapor and there is a "time to be born and a time to die." I only wish the church emphasized both scriptures when they pray for the healing of ninety-year-old people.

Death. It happens. Quite often actually.

As she went in one direction and I in the other, no one could have guessed she would not make it to lunch. Blood clots breaking loose and blocking a heart valve will do that to a person. Within an hour of my joke, which brought her unconfessed happiness, her body said "enough" just feet from where we had parted ways earlier in the day. She had walked the earth for barely three decades and one of the last things she did was laugh at one of my jokes. Some people offer money. Others offer food. I offered a joke.

The Bible also says, "No one knows what is coming." Since that's true, make someone laugh today. Or maybe offer some encouragement.

Because, who knows. They may walk in the opposite direction and it may be the last chance we'll ever have.

A Legacy in Death: (Ron)

Not long ago, I sat in the hospital room of my 49-year-old friend Ron. A life-long buddy, this was not our first visit since he became sick. When I first learned of his terminal diagnosis, I visited him in his home. I had decided that we should talk like men. None of this, "You're going to beat this, Ron."

Fact is, he wasn't going to beat the odds by being cured. He was going to die.

I arrived at his home and he greeted me warmly. We moseyed into his living room, sat down and began the important conversation. Within minutes he was trying to convince me he would overcome his disease and win the battle with cancer. Knowing, in advance, that I would bring candor to the conversation, I stepped up to the plate and swung for the fence called courage.

"Maybe the discussion we should have today Ron is not about changing a pre-determined outcome, but rather the leadership you have the opportunity to provide to your family during your last few weeks on earth." He agreed. So we talked about leaving behind a legacy of strength and courage.

The inevitable came just weeks later. "Steve, if you want to visit Ron one last time, you need to see him today." I went to the hospital and as I was about to leave his room that day, we held hands yet exchanged no words. Our last communication was limited to eye contact. Oh, we both could have spoken. We chose not to. A stare into each other's eyes was all that was needed. A life well lived on one side and a life continuing on the other. One man has finished the race, the other continuing along the course. One author completing his book, the other still writing. With chapters yet unknown. One man showing leadership in death. The other? He can only hope to become that kind of man.

Two boys meeting in the 70's with a lifetime still to be carved out. Two men, forty years later, saying goodbye. Words aren't needed. They have proven to each other they care. They will forever maintain a bond that life's challenges and disappointments can never destroy. Their eye contact is sufficient as a deeper connection exists. A simple and silent gaze speaks volumes. It is deafening to the only two who can hear it.

A tight squeeze of the hand was what we gave each other as I left that day and an acknowledgment of a lifetime friendship that will never be defeated by death. Fueled by a tough love discussion weeks earlier on leaving a legacy by how you should die.

Taking Action: (Jeff)
I grabbed a small basket as I entered the store and

proceeded to pick up a few items. It was a cold and rainy Colorado spring day and the only thing I wasn't in the mood for was to be outside. Doing anything. So a brief shopping excursion ruled the day.

"Hey, Big Guy," I heard as I wandered about. I turned and noticed a good friend of mine standing nearby. It had been a few months since I'd seen him. "Hey, Jeff! Good to see you!" I said. And I meant it. It was really good to see him. We always connected and had much in common. We shared laughs, stories…and gum. Jeff loved gum and always had a rich supply in his pocket.

We exchanged small talk and, minutes later, he broke the monotony with the proverbial, "We should get together real soon." He then asked for my phone number, but I'd had it with that trite and ineffective line, "Let's get together." People say it all the time and they rarely mean it. So I turned the tables on him.

"Let's do get together. I'd like that. Here's my number. But listen, I'm serious. Don't take my number if you're not going to call. For every ten people who take my number, I'm lucky if one ever calls."

"Okay," he said. "I'll call. I promise."

We wished each other well and said our goodbyes. We then promised we'd continue the conversation over a beer or a five mile run soon. The number. The promise. The plan. The same result…Nothing.

Sadly, however, on this occasion, our failure to deliver mattered because I did see Jeff again. Just a few weeks after our encounter in the store. I saw him at his funeral. All of his marathon training had not kept his heart from giving out at an early age. He now belonged to history and my number was packed away safely in his wallet. For history.

It's time to take the phone numbers out of our wallets and dial the phone, and it's time to get off of social media to laugh with someone over dinner. It's time to give a hug and a touch.

Just make sure it's a hug and a touch in life. And not a hug and a touch at the casket.

CHAPTER 11

RANDOM AND USELESS THOUGHTS
STUFF I SIMPLY COULDN'T THROW AWAY

~~~~~~~~~~~~~~~~~~~~~~~~~~~~~~~~~

- Who writes obituaries and is this stuff believable? Was Ralph really "loved by everyone he met" or did Carl really "brought a smile to everyone each time he entered the room"? Do we really know that Bonnie is now "dancing with Jesus"?

  To be fair, it is better than the alternative, "Sam was detested by all of his colleagues and thought to be a kiss up to the boss." Or, "Mary was known as the town whiner and disliked by most of the people who knew her."

- Got to love the obituaries of Christians. "For nineteen years, Bobby fought a courageous battle against cold sores and is now in the loving arms of Jesus." He is now "singing with the angels."

What about Satan worshipers? How does their obituary read? "Priscilla, known fondly to her friends as the Princess of Darkness, waged war against everything good and is now in the hate filled arms of the Devil and is chanting with the evil ones."

• I poured over the obituaries this morning and realized: There's a huge difference between what the obituary says and what it is trying to say:

It says: "Donald brought a smile to everyone in the room when he entered."
It Means: Because Donald's fly was usually open and his pants were usually five inches too short.

It says: "Trevor could fire up a room with his mere presence."
It means: After a night of drinking, light a match anywhere in his vicinity and the entire town would go up in flames.

It says: "Rob is in the loving arms of Jesus."
It means: Actually, he is bent over the knees of Jesus and the Savior is opening up a can of whoopass for all of the sinning Rob did.

It says: "Barbara gained her wings and flew to Heaven."
It means: Good to hear that wings have

replaced the horns Barbara sported for the last seven decades.

- Just this morning I read this in a local obituary: "She is survived by --- --- and the late ---- ----." Survived by someone who has died? That's noteworthy to be sure.

- Speaking of the use of the word late in referencing those who have passed. Take the biblical figure Lazarus who died and was brought back to life by Jesus. Is it the late Lazarus? Although he died, he later "un-died." So is he late or simply a surviving member of the family?

  "She is survived by the kind-of-late Lazarus but was also pre-deceased by...Lazarus."

  One can only envision the family obituaries after Lazarus died, yet again, a few years later...

  "She is pre-deceased by her late Uncle Lazarus, oops, survived by her Uncle Lazarus, oops, again, pre-deceased by her late Uncle Lazarus. But stay tuned. You never know with this guy!"

- Speaking of Lazarus. I wonder if he was upset when Jesus raised him from the dead. "What the heck, Jesus! Two minutes ago, I was walking along the golden streets of Heaven with the beautiful and made perfect Bathsheba, and now I have to live here again? Now, thanks to you, I get to die a second time?"

- Do our departed loved ones really look down from Heaven, observing our every good deed? After all, our sports heroes constantly remind us that "dear Grammy was watching from Heaven."Yikes!

  If Dear Ole Grammy in Heaven can see me playing ball, can she see me when I'm in the privacy of my home? Doing, uh, oh crap! I should have thought this through before I invited Grams in on my daily activities!

- A well-known actor died today. According to the news, the actor died of old age. I'm not sure how one dies of old age. I can only imagine that discussion.

  "I've got some good news and some bad news. First, the bad news. You are going to die of old age. Now the good news. You lived long enough to die of old age."

- Well that's odd. I just found my brother's website. It is still active although he died nearly fifteen years ago. It gives me a window of what he was thinking during his last days.
  It may very well be the last active reminder of him.

  I'll visit the site more often.

- The greatest bargain in the history of mankind? The postage stamp. Even now, for roughly fifty cents, I can give a piece of correspondence to the carrier and he will take it across the country and deliver it directly to the door of the recipient. There's only one problem. Who uses snail-mail anymore?

- Watching a crime show investigating a murder from 1978. Showing the original film footage of the crime, the license plate on the vehicle is blotted out. Is that really necessary? Is someone really going to steal the identity of plates issued thirty years ago?

- You gotta love the Cuban accents of those women in Miami. They can make anything sound hot! They simply utter the words "inflamed hemorrhoids" and half of the guys in the area start falling in love!

- How can some people drain you of all of your energy simply by saying they would like to have coffee with you?

- Have you ever noticed that the people who teach love, tolerance, forgiveness, peace and understanding the most are the least likely people in the community who will give you those things?

- Lee Greenwood was singing "God Bless the USA" at a political rally and many in the crowd had out raised hands as they sang along. It was identical to the scene you would encounter at church on Sunday. Enjoying a historic and patriotic song is commendable yet it may be a stretch to equate it with a song of spiritual worship or praise.

- Phrases that have outlived their welcome and need to go:

"You go, girl." (Usually spoken by a non-athlete who somehow believe this is motivational to any female),

"Take a chill pill." (Spoken by a person losing an argument to an impassioned and well informed debater.)

"Let me be clear." (You pretty much know whatever follows these words are full of lies, deceit, and horse manure)

"At the end of the day," (This stopped being cool at the end of the last decade)

"You know what I'm sayin'?" (Actually, I don't. You read that on my face and that's why you had to ask.)

"Does that make sense?" (Where have the people gone who have confidence in their speech and ability to clearly articulate a thought?)

- Next election, I'm doing something different when I go to the polls. I'm voting for gridlock. That's right, gridlock. If the Republicans are looking at full control, I'll vote Democrat, and vice-versa. Gridlock is the way to go.

Why? I figure, that with split control, nothing will get done and when these jokers get nothing done in D.C., have you noticed how better off our lives are? It's a fact. For a better America, vote for gridlock!

- It must be selective boldness on the part of our politically correct culture. Case in point, a television news anchor announces he's gay and wins praise from the national media for the courage it took to speak up. Yet football star Tim Tebow publically shares his faith in Jesus and he is mocked by the same media, scorned, and told he should remain silent on the subject. The intolerance of the tolerant. You don't suspect any bigotry here do you?

- The ad read, "Quite possibly the most comfortable and functional underwear on earth." I get comfortable, but what in heaven's name makes for "functional" underwear? I mean, really. Can underwear ever not "function"? I can see it now:

"Mr. Bonham, you're late for your jury duty assignment."

"Yeah. I'm feeling you, Judge. But on the way here, my drawz malfunctioned, causing me to be late."

"Well, Mr. Bonham, I suggest that you invest into functioning butt huggers in the future."

"Word up, homie."

- If people drove to church as fast as they do

when they leave church, we wouldn't have 30% of the congregation straggling through the doors fifteen minutes late.

- Ever noticed how people who think the rules don't apply to them also think the consequences of breaking those rules don't apply to them either?

- People will love your strength and honesty but will equally dislike your... strength and honesty.

- Never grow close to someone you will eventually need to separate from. But how do you know?

- It takes an hour to accept someone into your life and often years to remove them if needed.

- Nothing beats the awkward and forced smile of a relative when you tell them about the healthy bonus you received at Christmas.

- I saw an ad. "Mature Men Wanted." I figured I'd better keep turning the pages until I found a better fit.

- Some people spend their life making themselves look better while others spend their life making themselves be better.

- That awkward moment when you are at a friend's house watching the game, they give you a coaster for your drink and you realize the coaster is probably worth more than the table they are trying to protect.

- A Hollywood actress recently had her breasts removed out of fear of getting breast cancer. So that's why our elected officials in Washington are so nutless. Most of them must be afraid of getting testicular cancer.

- Wouldn't it be nice, if the good news in your life traveled as quickly amongst your enemies as the bad news in your life does?

- Where would we be today, if we would have walked through every open door of opportunity that was presented to us along the way?

- To the words thank you: Where, oh where, have you gone?

- In the average class of high school graduates, what's the percentage of them who will ever create a job during the course of their career? 5%? 2%? Less than 1%?

  Whatever the number, they will certainly be in the minority and will have decades of heavy tax burden, negative media portrayal and jealousy from many people. In short, job creators aren't often popular, regardless of the good they do for others.

- Roughly 50% of Americans pay almost no income tax. Remind me again. It's the rich who aren't paying their fair share?

- It's kind of strange how people don't have time

all year long to do their taxes but their schedule miraculously clears up every April 14 and 15?

- What can be said about those people who get excited over receiving a refund and think they pulled a fast one over on the IRS? They believe their overpayment is a gift from Uncle Sam. WTH! I can hear them now: "I don't mind paying taxes. In fact, the last two years I've received money back!"

- When the TV preacher says, "Please consider offering a love gift today," he means:

  "I don't care if it's a love gift, a gift out of guilt, a gift stemming from hate and disgust, or paying a fine for your sins. Just contribute, baby!"

- Things you see today in our leaders that you can't find in history: Winston Churchill blaming his challenges and failures on a cable news network. Yet that's what I saw the President do today. True leadership has taken a severe hit the past seventy years.

- When thumbing through the TV guide, I see that Crocodile Hunter (Repeat) is on tonight. Is the notification Repeat really necessary information? Since the real croc hunter left us years ago. I'm thinking that a new episode is out of the question at this point.

- Why do people want fat wallets and thin bodies yet continue to eat constantly while sitting in the living room recliner?

- Why are cadets at the Air Force Academy dismissed if caught lying and/or cheating and yet their boss, the Commander-in-Chief (either party), lies constantly and is never held accountable for those falsehoods? Why is the bar of honesty and integrity held higher for the twenty year old cadet than the leader of the free world?

- Why is a Kindergarten student suspended for kissing his friend on the hand and yet Congress is filled with sexual harassment at the highest levels without consequence? Why is the bar of decency held higher for the five year old student than the elected officials who run our country?

- With thousands of years of history for our review, why do people still believe that something will be provided to them for free? Just a few moments of thought would reveal that everything comes at a cost to someone.

- The ugliest and most disgusting place on earth is a men's locker room.

- If I had a choice, I'd prefer that God not help me find my cars keys. I'd rather he help me avoid an accident instead.

- Why do commercial airline pilots wear hats? Does it really get breezy enough in the cockpit to require headwear?

- It's a travesty that most bathrooms have 150 square feet of mirror space and 2 square inches of fan space. All the women are saying, "Right on." and all the men are telling their girlfriends, "Careful what you wish for, babe. One day we'll share the same bathroom!"

- The Bible praises a person for using few words and celebrates brevity. Yet the Bible is 66 books long and repeats itself over and over. Not sure why four gospels were needed telling the same stories. If the Statute of Limitations on plagiarism is less than 2000 years, a couple of those writers are breathing easier.

- When someone gets slightly hurt and is writhing in pain, screaming and crying, what's the Statute of Limitations on the time before you can laugh at them and imitate the dance they did after they stubbed their toe? I know that mocking within five minutes is too soon. What about a day?

- Who came up with the idea of burning things as an acceptable way to protest or show displeasure with something? I'm thinking the credit belongs to God. Don't forget. When he finally "had it up to here" with Sodom & Gomorrah, what did he do? He started setting things on fire. Everything. He lit that sucker up like a Christmas tree.

And where is God's final destination for those who don't make the grade? They spend eternity in a lake of fire. A fiery furnace. Fire and brimstone. Why was fire God's way to punish unbelievers for ever and ever?

Why not another way to punish them like, "You blew it and now you're going to hell. You have to listen to Michael Bolton sing forever. You'll live in New Jersey, eating government mandated school lunches."

- Maybe, in the future, God can duplicate the burning bush feat he accomplished with Moses. Even though God torched the bush, it was not consumed. Hey, there's a solution. Feeling the need to riot? Light a police car on fire and it won't be consumed. It just burns and burns. Something tells me this would take the fun out of rioting.

- Speaking of fire. What was up with burning bras? Were women thinking this would change the minds of men?

  "We women are going to protest for equal rights by burning our bras!!!!" The men saw this and huddled around scheming, "Our plan worked guys. Now what can we do to make them burn their panties in anger as well?"

- People demand respect, but they don't respect demands.

- I'm pretty sure, that in order to get a job holding a sign for a road construction crew, the main qualification must be the ability to smoke all day long. After all, do you ever see a sign holder on a road construction project that doesn't have a smoke hanging out of their mouth?

"What's that? You don't smoke? I'm sorry, sir, we don't have any job openings at this time."

- Road rage is at an all-time high. In fact, I'm fairly sure that the old bumper sticker, "Honk if you love Jesus," has been replaced by the bumper sticker, "Honk with the hand not currently flipping me off."

- Is it a requirement that to be named Cleo one must be a fortune teller? Have you ever met a pastor's wife named Cleo? Huh? Have ya?!?!

- Corniest song ever recorded? "Seasons in the Sun," a 1973 tear jerker by Terry Jacks. "Goodbye, Papa, it's hard to die, when all the birds are singing in the sky…."

- Painful on the ears. Not to be outdone, the "B" side of that 45 record was the 2nd corniest song ever recorded… "Put the Bone In," a song about a woman asking her butcher to put in the bone with the rest of her meat order. You can't make this stuff up.

REFERENCES

CHAPTER 1:
"Time and chance" (Ecclesiastes 9:11)
"Better a dry crust with peace and quiet than a house full
of feasting with strife," (Proverbs 17:1)

CHAPTER 2:
"A time for …" (Ecclesiastes 3:1ff)

CHAPTER 3:
Leon Fuller quote (http://archives.chicagotribune.
com/1984/10/07/page/46/article/west-southwest)
"As a man thinketh" (Proverbs 23:7)
" God's children begging bread" (Psalm 37:25)

CHAPTER 4:
Edward Spencer story (Various including http://wesclark.
com/burbank/did_i_do_my_best.html and http://archives.
chicagotribune.com/1960/09/04/page/37/article/the-or-
deal-of-edward-spencer)
"What you sow is what you reap" (Galatians 6:7)
"I was young and now I am old" (Psalm 37:25)

CHAPTER 5:
"Therefore I tell you, whatever you ask in prayer, believe
that you have received it, and it will be yours." (Mark 11:24)
"If you abide in me, and my words abide in you, ask whatever you wish, and it will be done for you." (John 15:7)
"Ask, and it will be given to you" (Matthew 7:7)
"…so that whatever you ask the Father in my name, he may
give it to you" (John 15:16)

"Call to me, and I will answer you…" (Jeremiah 33:3)

"And whatever we ask we receive from him…" (1 John 3:22)

"Before they call I will answer; while they are yet speaking I will hear" (Isiah 65:24)

"And whatever you ask in prayer, you will receive, if you have faith" (Matthew 21:22)

"Truly, truly, I say to you, whatever you ask of the Father in my name, he will give it to you" (John 16:23)

"When you pray" (Matthew 6:6)

CHAPTER 6:

Hillary Clinton claims (http://www.politifact.com/truth-o-meter/statements/2016/jul/19/mitch-mcconnell/did-hillary-clinton-lie-about-being-named-after-si/)

CHAPTER 8:

"Tempted as we are" (Hebrews 4:15)

"Peace be still" (Mark 4:39)

"Do you not know that those who run in a race all run" (1 Corinthians 9:24)

CHAPTER 9:

Entertaining angels unaware (Hebrews 13:2)

CHAPTER 10:

"Time to be born and a time to die" (Ecclesiastes 3:2)

"No one knows what is coming." (Matthew 24:36)

ACKNOWLEDGMENTS:

I'm eternally grateful to so many people in my life:

To those who supported and showed me a better way when I was trying to find one: Greg Bonham, Kinney Neel, Rick Kness, Kevin & Colleen Westhuis, Dennis Sumner, Paul & Karen Folger, Tim Shea, Nate Treanor and Dik & Angie Pittman.

To the most wonderful ladies in the world. All of you are the definition of class and have my full respect: Jill Christensen, Crista Huff, Daphne Huscroft, Stacy Petty, Lesley Lang, Jacci Peterson, Dianne Morris, Jill Davis, Anne Marlow, Tina Beth, Sheri Szabatura, Jenny Novoryta, Jean Reilly, Deanne Weiss, Jennifer Piehl Barker, Amanda Enloe and Mimi Foster.

And to Aly and Caleb's second set of parents. A young married couple can never have too much love and support and I appreciate all of you: Jerry & Lori Bond and Gary & Laura Lei Albert.

www.ingramcontent.com/pod-product-compliance
Lightning Source LLC
Chambersburg PA
CBHW070826120626
46556CB00002B/662